# The Next Revolution

Morris Malone came suddenly to his feet and began pacing up and down the room. The other two watched him, frowning their puzzlement.

He stopped suddenly and looked at them. He said, surprise in his voice, "You know, we've just been horsing around. Just kidding. But you know what? I'm beginning to think it might work."

# TRAMPLE AN EMPIRE DOWN

Mack Reynolds

LEISURE BOOKS • NEW YORK CITY

A LEISURE BOOK

Published by

Nordon Publications, Inc.
Two Park Avenue
New York, N.Y. 10016

*One Man with a dream, at pleasure,*
*Shall go forth and conquer a crown;*
*And three with a new song's measure*
*Can trample an empire down.*

—Arthur W.E. O'Shaughnessy

# 1

Morris Malone was unhappy. His latest attempt to get a job had fallen flat on its face, as always. He had educated himself to teach history, and while still in school the profession was automated—ultra-mated, they were beginning to call it these days—out from under him. With the coming of television and Tri-Di, and of the National Data Banks, the old form of teaching, was passé. No more, a teacher sitting before a few dozen students in a school classroom.

He didn't deny that the new system was more practical. In the past, the teacher had to address himself to the average pupil in the class. Those that were slow failed to understand, and those who were bright were bored. Today, in his own home, the pupil could go as fast or as slowly as he wished, consulting by phone screen, when necessary, the tutor who had been assigned him in that particular subject. It didn't apply to some subjects of course, such as laboratory sciences or physical education, but it applied with a vengeance to history. There were tens of thousands of canned lectures, on every level, and hundreds of thousands of books, in the National Data Banks teaching section. Only a handful of history teachers held down jobs, and they were selected by the computers on the basis of their ability quotients.

He sighed and stared out the window of his small suburban house. As far as the eye could see there were almost identical houses. A somewhat ant-like existence, he thought. But at least it was better than living in a high-rise apartment house in a pseudo-city.

Morris Malone was in his early thirties and he had never heard of the other, but he strikingly resembled Henry Fonda at the same age. Right now, he was on the disgruntled side because he couldn't think of anything he wanted to do that fitted in with his financial situation. He was tired of reading, just recently having got off his binge of cramming in hopes of getting a job specializing in the Napoleonic Period of French history. He felt he could recite the whole life story of the Little Corsican. Not that it had done him any good. The computers had passed him by with great élan.

He could have watched Tri-Di but he hated canned entertainment.

Jack Zieglar, hands in pockets, came sauntering down the street and up the walk. Morris Malone went over to the door and let him in.

If Morris Malone resembled Henry Fonda, then Jack Zieglar was the image of Marlon Brando in his earlier days. Marlon Brando playing one of his easier-going parts. Zieglar took life slow and philosophically, and a bit drunkenly.

He said, "Cheers, Mo. What spins?"

"Not a damn thing," Malone said, leading the way back to the living room. "What spins with you?" He slumped down onto the couch.

His friend sank into a chair and said, "I came over

to see if you've got enough pseudo-dollars left this month to spring me a drink or two."

Morris Malone came back to his feet and went over to the autobar, pulling his Universal Credit Card from an inner pocket.

"Beer?"

"Yeah."

"I'll have one too, I guess." He put the credit card in the bar's payment slot, put his thumb print on the identification screen and dialed two dark beers. When they came he returned to his guest.

Jack said, "How'd you do with Napoleon?"

"I met my Waterloo."

The identity screen on the door buzzed and Morris looked up. It was his other close buddy, Jed Kleiser. Morris was too lazy to get up. He touched a button on the phone screen and the door opened.

Jed came in and looked at them. He said, "Who in hell's still got enough credit left to buy beer? It's three days before the monthly Guaranteed Annual Income payment."

Morris Malone let martyrdom come into his face but he got up again and went over to his autobar and put his credit card in the slot, his thumbprint on the tiny identification screen and dialed another beer.

A metalic computer voice said, "You have insufficient credit for this order."

Morris stared down at the bar in disgust. "I didn't know I was that broke," he said. He went back to the couch, where the newcomer had already taken a seat at the far end from where Mo had been sitting. "Sorry, Jed."

Jed shrugged. He was a tallish type, somewhat gangling, and, though less than handsome, had that boy-next-door look that an amazing number of women liked. He was roughly the same age as the others.

Jack said, "This is a helluva world for an aspiring alcoholic to live in. The ultra-welfare state, People's Capitalism. Ha! Guaranteed Annual Income. Just enough not to starve on, but not enough to enjoy yourself."

Jed said mildly, "It's not so bad. We all three ought to get married. Then we'd have three mopsies also getting their GAI. Share the cost of a house and so forth."

"Yeah," Jack said, without interest. "And then have a couple of kids and they'd both get half a monthly payment until eighteen. The only trouble is, I'm a satyr and like to play the field. Having only one woman would send me around the bend."

"People's Capitalism," Morris said, sipping carefully at his beer, since it was going to have to last. "Actually, what it amounts to is charity for the majority, but the powers that be still control the country, and the rich get richer but the poor stay about the same. The businessmen, the politicians, the churches, in short, the Establishment, do fine, but it's tough titty for the rest of us."

"So what can you do about it, Mo?" Jed shrugged.

Out of a clear sky, Morris Malone took the first step. He said sourly, "What this country needs is a revolution."

The other two took that in.

He said definitely, "The country's gone flat. No more wars, no more depressions, and with ultramation and computerization, practically nobody works. Practically everybody's on Guaranteed Annual Income. Even the space program has gotten into a rut, with nothing exciting going on. Practically everybody just sits around taking trank or drinking beer and watching Tri-Di like a bunch of idiots. The whole country's in a mental slump."

"And?" the other two said in unison.

"We need a revolution, that's what. There hasn't been a revolution in this country for well over two hundred years. The nation's ripe for it."

Jack said, just for the sake of saying something, "What kind of a revolution?"

Morris looked at him as though the question was foolish. "What'd'ya mean what kind of a revolution? One that'd wind up with us three on top of the heap. The leaders of revolutions that win always wind up in the catbird seat. Look at Mussolini, look at Franco, Tito, Chiang Kai-shek, Lenin, Hitler's gang, Napoleon, even Mao in China. And most of the leaders of the American revolution started off rich to begin with, but wound up richer."

"Oh, great. Wizard," Jack said, working away at his own beer, though noting sadly that it was already two-thirds gone. "But the trouble is, most of these revolutionist types wind up getting clobbered."

"I don't know," Morris argued. "They always start off telling the people, usually the poor people, how dedicated they are, how altruistic. Their hearts bleed for the downtrodden. But then, when they come to power, they start living it up like kings, and, as often as not, the man in the street is at least as bad off as he ever was."

"Yeah, but usually your revolutionist leaders, even the successful ones, wind up getting nailed," Jack said.

"Oh, I don't know. Stalin, Tito, Franco, Mao, Salazar, of Portugal, all died in bed at ripe old ages.

So did most of the American revolutionists, except Burr and Hamilton. Napoleon died in bed, for that matter, although he was in exile. But take even those who were clobbered, like Mussolini. He started off as a poor editor of a third rate, so-called socialist newspaper. He came to power as a fascist in the early 1920s and stayed in, living in luxury, exerting power, until 1945. Hell, he had almost a quarter of a century living it up. When he was finally killed he was an old man. Do you think if he had his druthers, that he would have switched lives?"

Jed yawned and said, "Well, it's a wizard of an idea, but three men can't start a revolution."

Morris Malone finished his beer. He said, argumentatively, "Why not? How many does it take to start? I sometimes think that Voltaire started the French Revolution all by his lonesome. All right, by the time it came along, he was dead, but he started the ball rolling."

Jed said thoughtfully, "The American Revolution really got started by only about three men; Sam Adams, Patrick Henry, James Otis."

Jack said, "I thought it was George Washington, Benjamin Franklin, those guys."

"They came in later. Got on the bandwagon because they had to. Hell, that old bastard Franklin didn't come in until almost the end, when the fat was already in the fire. He wanted to compromise with the king. The patriots should have shot him."

Jack said to Morris, "You've got to have some kind of program to get the people stirred up. You just can't come out and say we three are going to take over the country, so that we can live it up."

Morris thought about that. He said finally, "We've got to put it on a high moral level. And something really different to wow them. Something radically opposite from what we have now."

"Yeah, Jed said, "But what, Mo?"

Morris snapped his fingers in inspiration and said, "How's this for a basic slogan: *Less Production! Lower the Gross National Product!*"

The other two eyed him as though he had just left the world of reason.

"Have you gone drivel-happy?" Jack snorted. "The demand for the past century and more has been to up the Gross National Product, the Per Capita National Income. Avoid a depression. Cut down on unemployment."

"It's a lot of curd," Morris said. "Unemployment isn't a problem, it's a way of life. We're using up half of the world's raw materials and flushing about two thirds of it down the drain. Just take one item, advertising. We'd advocate eliminating it. It doesn't produce a damn worthwhile thing."

"Every newspaper and magazine in the country would go broke," Jed protested.

"Great. Let 'em go broke. At the rate they're publishing tripe, we won't have a tree left in the country in a few years. Let people get their news on Tri-Di or on their library booster screens from the National Data Banks. So far as magazines are concerned, who'd miss 'em? There's only a dozen in the country worth reading anyway and most of them not dependent upon advertising. Think of all the wood pulp and man hours of labor you'd save if you kicked out advertising." He considered it. "Let all signs go at the same time, especially neon signs and billboards. What the hell good are signs? They're the most garish thing in our culture."

Jack protested mildly. "If you want to buy

something, they tell you where it is."

"Curd. If you're in your own neighborhood you know where the stores are with the things you want. If you're somewhere else, you can ask the locals, or look it up in the phone book."

The other two considered it.

"Holy Jumping Zoroaster," Jed said. "It'd save a lot of paper and a lot of other material. And it'd save a lot of power, turning all those damned signs off."

"That's just the beginning on this Produce Less program," Morris said. "We're going to end planned obsolescence. Take cars. American hovercars are designed to start falling apart, or being out of style, after 30,000 miles, or about three years. After that length of time, any driver who can afford it begins to think in terms of a new car. His hovers are going, repairs needed, an engine job, there are dents and scratches in the finish. And he looks like a bum driving a vehicle that's out of style. As far back as the Model T and Model A Fords, a car was built to last at least ten years. A German Volkswagen, when they first came out, was expected to last 150,000 miles and a Mercedes 300,000. And the styles didn't change enough to make any difference. And both of them got better mileage than American cars. I won't even mention the Jap cars. Now, what we'd do is prohibit any car that weighed more than a ton. No cars could have more than four cylinders and all would have to give at least forty miles to the gallon. No power steering, no power brakes, no power windows. What the hell good are they? And we wouldn't allow batteries that were deliberately designed to wear out in a year or eighteen months. Lead is too damned valuable. Any scientist or engineer who came up with some scheme for planned obsolescence, we'd toss in the slammer.

"And that's just the beginning," Morris continued, in full voice now. "Take electric light bulbs. They're manufactured now with the built-in expectation of lasting approximately one thousand hours. Hell, they've got the knowhow to make light bulbs that would last the life of the house. It applies all the way down the line. In our grandfathers' day a man would buy a suit, and when he died, they'd alter it a bit and his son would take it over. How long does a suit last now? Two or three years?"

Jack said, thoughtfully, "Yeah. You could go on with a lot of examples. Take packaging. What the hell good is most of it? My grandfather once told me that when he was a kid, soap used to sit on the shelves of a store without even a wrapper. Now it comes wrapped in tissue paper, then in a heavier wrapper, all fancied up, and then in a cardboard carton, along with a couple score other bars of soap. Look at all the paper used."

Jed said, also thoughtfully, "Yeah. And all the artists, and layout men, and printers and so forth. All turning out something of no use."

Jack said, "What'd we call this party?"

And Morris said, "The Subversive Party."

"Are you completely around the bend? The IBI would have us before the day was out."

"No, no. I told you, we'd have to wow them. Shock 'em. Something really different. There's nothing wrong with subversion. All it means is to overthrow something in existence. To change. There's nothing in the American Constitution against subversion. Just so you do it legally. No force and violence. You have to get the majority of the people to vote for it. For instance, in the old days, before the Republicans and Democrats merged, when they had an election, if the Republicans were in, then when the election came, by definition the Democrats were trying to subvert the Republicans. But the word became kind of a taboo. So-called socialists, like Norman Thomas, never referred to themselves as subversives, not even the more radical Socialist Labor Party. Hell, not even the Commies or the Trotskyites. But we'll come right out and call ourselves the Subversive Party. However, we'll advocate coming to power by democratic procedure. We'll vote ourselves in, and once in we'll dump the present version of democracy."

"We will?" Jed said.

"Sure, it doesn't work. Democracy is the ideal government, admittedly. But it only works among peers. When you have a situation where any semiliterate, moron can arrive at age eighteen and have as good a vote as an Einstein, then it's nonsense. Democracy, in America, became a farce more than a century ago. Even presidents were elected because of their TV image, or some such. The candidate with the most dollars to spend for TV appearances, newspaper ads and so on, made it. The voters, on average, conducted themselves like idiots. Do you realize that even Nixon, at the nadir of his disaster, had something like a quarter of the country pulling for him? If some of those people had caught him with his hand in their pocket, they still would have voted for him."

Morris Malone came suddenly to his feet and began pacing up and down the room. The other two watched him, frowning their puzzlement.

He stopped suddenly and looked at them. He said, surprise in his voice, "You know, we've just been horsing around. Just kidding. But you know what? I'm beginning to think it might work."

# 2

Jack snorted a laugh.

"No. I mean it," Morris said.

Jed said, "Holy Zoroaster, Mo, you can't start a political party without money. And we're all three on Guaranteed Annual Income."

"Yes, you can. You can start it on peanuts, if you've got a program that fits the needs of the country. Or, at least, you can convince the people you have. Look at Lenin's gang, a few months before they came to power. Half of them were in exile or prison in Siberia, the rest were on their uppers in Switzerland or somewhere else abroad. Trotsky was half starving in New York, cadging meals."

"Well," Jack argued, "how would we start?"

"In a few days, we get our monthly GAI payments. We'll all three tighten our belts and put fifty pseudo-dollars into the kitty, the treasury of the Subversive Party. With it we'll buy stationary, print up membership application blanks, and rent a post office box."

"Then what?" Jed said grudgingly.

"Then we start writing letters, under a dozen different pseudonyms, to every newspaper and magazine in the country that prints a *Letters to the Editor* column. And we send out press releases to every paper and Tri-Di news commentator on the air telling them about the formation of the new party."

"Hell," Jack growled. "They wouldn't give us any publicity."

"Sure they will. All of those characters grasp at straws when it comes to news. They're short of it. There hasn't been a war for a coon's age. The space program is routine now. Most crime has disappeared with the Universal Credit Card and all banking being taken care of by the National Data Banks' banking section. Without money, most crime is impractical. At any rate, we'll be news. After a time, we'll probably have chances to appear on Tri-Di programs. Guest speakers, debates, interviews, that sort of thing. After we get going as a political party, we'll demand equal time every occasion a Democratic Republican gives a speech."

Jack said, "That's great. But it's hardly a beginning. You've got to have pseudo-dollars on hand to print leaflets, pamphlets, maybe bring out a newspaper, rent halls for meetings. Where do we raise money?"

"A lot of ways," Morris told him. "We'll charge five pseudo-dollars to join the Party, and five dollars dues each month. We'll announce ourselves a legal party and demand credit exchangers from the National Data Banks banking section so that we can transfer dues and donations into an account for the Subversive Party. It'll be in our names. We're the National Executive Committee, the Triumvirate that heads the Party and makes all decisions."

Jed was becoming intrigued. "How else can we raise pseudo-dollars?"

"Well, for one thing, as soon as the name and program gets out a bit, we're going to be infiltrated by the Inter-Continental Bureau of Investigation, and probably other government organizations, including the Center City police. They'll undoubtedly try to bribe one or more of us. They always do. Back in the twenties there were so many F.B.I. men in the American Communist Party that a judge up in New England threw out a case, claiming that the Communist Party was a branch of the Federal Government and he had no jurisdiction to prosecute the government."

"But if we let government agents in, won't they be able to ferret out our secrets?" Jed scowled.

But Morris had him there. He said triumphantly, "We won't have any secrets. It will drive them around the bend, and lead them to working still more agents in, with more bribes, and every one having to pay his entry membership fee and his dues."

Ideas were coming to Morris by the dozen.

He said, "And we'll do what the Nazis used to do. Each membership will have a number. Ours will be, one, two, and three; the founders of the Party. Members who have low numbers will have prestige, since they joined up when the Party was in its infancy. After Hitler came to power, everybody in Germany wanted a low number membership card in the National Socialist Party. And the Nazi bigwigs made a killing selling them. That's what we'll do. We'll *start* the first memberships out at number one thousand. Then, when we get larger, we'll sell the lower numbered memberships to people who are anxious to get on the band wagon."

Jack looked at him in admiration and shook his head. "What a mind," he said.

Morris looked at him thoughtfully. "You did a hitch in the army, didn't you?"

"Yeah, worst luck."

"What rank did you have?"

"I ended up a corporal."

"Wizard. Hitler was a corporal. You can be the head of our Storm Troopers."

"Storm Troopers!" Jed blurted.

"Sure. It's a great draw for teenagers and young cloddies in general. They get to strut around in front of the mopsies in their uniforms. They'll join up like crazy."

Jack said plaintively, "I was in the army but all I did was put cans on the PX shelves."

"Who'll know? Although we'll call you—affectionately— The Corporal, we'll drop hints around that really you were a general. Now what we need is a name and a shirt."

The other two looked at him.

"We can't call them Storm Troopers," he said. "That'd leave a bad taste in people's mouths. They'll be the equivalent of the German *Steel Helm*, or the American Legion in the States, though precious few of them will probably be veterans. We can call them Minute Men, after the original Minute Men of the first American Revolution."

Jed scowled and said, "It seems to me that somebody else came up with that a few decades ago."

"That doesn't make any difference. It's a good name. Now what kind of special shirt and uniform can we use? We can't use brown shirts, Hitler loused that up, nor black, that was Mussolini; they both stink in people's memories."

"How about grey shirts?" Jack said, getting into the spirit of the thing. "We could sort of work it into our general program. The situation of the country is grey."

"No." Morris shook his head. "The Howard Scott Technocrats used grey back in the 1930s, and it's too drab, anyway."

Jed snorted and said, "How about No-Shirts? They could go around in kind of field jackets like Mao's communists back in the old days."

Morris shook his head again. "No. Peron, down in Argentina, used no-shirts. His first wife, Evita, used to address their followers as her poor shirtless-ones. Besides, we want something colorful."

Jack hit on it. "Suede shirts. Very masculine. In the tradition of Daniel Boone and Davy Crockett. Maybe with leather strings, or whatever they were, dangling from them. And the rest of the uniform of the Minute Men would be black leather pants and black leather jackets."

Morris had gotten a paper pad and a stylo and was making notes. "We're going to have to line up some clothing manufacturers and get a kickback for every article they sell our boys. Zoroaster, every young funker in the country, with nothing else to do, will want to join up so he can wear the shirt and roar around with the others on hoverbikes. Which reminds me. We'll have to line up some hoverbike manufacturer to put out a special Subversive Party hoverbike painted a light brown simulated suede. We'll get a kickback on each one, say a hundred pseudo-dollars per vehicle."

Jack said, "But what do these Minute Men do?"

"Nothing," Morris Malone told him. "We don't want a bunch of goons. We're strictly legitimate. They participate in our parades. They act as traffic directors at our rallies and ushers at our inside meetings."

He looked at Jed Kleiser thoughtfully, "You went to school, didn't you?"

"Sure, of sorts."

"What do you mean, of sorts? In what line? You got a degree, didn't you?"

"Yeah, I took a master's in economics. Damn little good it did me. How you can computerize economics Zoroaster only knows. But they seem to have."

"All right. You'll head our think tanks."

"What think tanks? You can't have a think tank with only one member. By definition, it's a whole collection of egg-heads."

"Oh, they'll come in like flies to a pile of manure. Being a member of a think tank is a status symbol. All double-domes want to belong to a think tank. Gives them prestige. You can start off, as soon as we get our stationery, and write the more far-out professors, over at the university, telling them they have been selected to join the think tank of the new political party, to help think out the nation's problems. When you get more than twenty in your first one, we'll start another, possibly in some other city, and when it's full, another. We'll wind up with most of the whiskers in the country."

Jed said cautiously, "What'll they think about?"

"What do we care? Anything they come up with. We'll file all their reports in the wastebasket. That's what happens to the product of the cerebral activities of most think tanks. They'll be non-profit, no salary attached. Just the prestige. In fact, they'll be like everybody else, they'll have to pony up their entrance fee and party dues."

Jack said, his beer long gone, "I wish the hell we had, between us, enough credit to buy a round of drinks."

Morris came to his feet. "I think I've got half a bottle of tequila I bought when I was down in Mexico."

"Now he tells us," Jack said. "This drivel-happy conversation has got me so dry my tongue is hanging out so it looks like a red necktie."

Morris went out to his kitchenette to return in a couple of minutes with three small glasses and a half-full litre of clear liquid.

They watched him, entranced, as he poured them each a double shot. He handed them around and then stood in toast. "To the revolution," he said.

Jack Zieglar said, "Look, I'm the head of the storm troopers that don't storm, and Jed, here, is head of the think tanks that don't think. What are you?"

Morris Malone looked at him in self-deprecation. "Isn't it obvious? I'm the Party theoretician. Like Karl Marx, like Lenin, like Robespierre, like Tom Paine..."

"All right, all right," Jack growled, tossing back the liquid H-Bomb.

# 3

Cliff Dix was mystified. He had been called back from his Florida vacation with a full week to go. The fishing on the St. Johns river was some of the best left in the country and he'd been having the time of his life. The large mouth bass were the biggest he had ever encountered. What with the pollution of almost every river and lake in the nation, fishing was hard to come by these days.

Now he drove his sports hovercar down the ramp which led to the parking area in the enormous government building which was his destination.

Cliff Dix was in his late twenties and looked, if anything, even younger. He was slim of build, light of hair, pale blue of eye, and when he'd been a kid he'd had to scrap more than once to defend himself from the nickname "baby face". It was possibly that early background that had made him, despite appearance, aggressive when pushed, almost to the point of belligerence. He took little from anyone. Yes, it was possibly that childhood that had led to his present occupation. He most certainly didn't *look* like an Inter-Continental Bureau of Investigation agent.

He climbed out of his vehicle before the elevator banks, dispatched it to park itself, and then went over to one of the identification booths. There were two uniformed officers there.

Cliff said to one of them, "Hello, Marvin. I've got an appointment with the Chief."

"Identification card, please."

Cliff sighed, even as he brought it forth. He said, "How many times do I have to pass this check station before you recognize me?" He put the card in the proper slot and then his right thumb print on the proper square.

A metalic computer voice said, "Identity verified," and he repossessed the card and returned it to an inner pocket.

The officer said, "You know how it is, Mr. Dix. Routine. Not even Mr. Hardenberg gets into this building without being checked out. Suppose the KGB or some other Soviet Complex outfit wanted to get in and put some operatives through plastic surgery and all so he'd be able to pass as one of our men."

"Ha," Cliff said. "Why in the hell would the KGB want to get a man in here? There's nothing worth learning. This bureau hasn't done anything worth doing for decades. I wish we were back in the days of Johnny Dillinger, Pretty Boy Floyd, Alvin Karpis."

He turned and approached an express elevator, entered it and said to the screen, "Twentieth Floor."

He had to bend his knees to accomodate to the acceleration. Twentieth floor, yet. How in the name of the Holy Jumping Zoroaster had the bureau ever gotten to the size that it could fill a building this size? Every year that went by Congress voted it a bigger budget and every year that went by there was less for it to do.

At the twentieth floor he got out and approached one of the three reception desks.

He said to the nattily outfitted girl there, "Agent

Clifford Dix. I'm supposed to have an appointment with Mr. Hardenberg."

"Identification, please," she trilled.

He put his I.D. card in the slot, his thumbprint on the screen. "Identity verified," the screen said.

"Should I summon an escort, Mr. Dix?"

"I know the way," Cliff said.

In actuality, Cliff Dix had been in this rarified area of the IBI building exactly once before, when he had received his credentials from the Chief, upon graduation from the IBI school. But he remembered the directions.

He made his way down corridors and finally wound up before the identity screen of an elaborate door. There was a man stationed to one side of it who looked him up and down but said nothing. The door opened and Cliff went on through.

He was in a medium sized office room, with six desks, occupied by three men, three women. Only one of the girls looked up and she was stationed before the door to the inner sanctum sanctorium. Cliff wondered how the other five managed to keep busy. What was there for them to keep busy at?

He went over to the reception desk and said, "Agent Clifford Dix. I believe that I have an appointment with Mr. Hardenberg."

"Yes, you have, Mr. Dix. In fact, you are five minutes late."

He looked at her sardonically. "I had to come up all the way from Florida."

She did the things that receptionists do and finally looked up at him and said, "The director will see you now."

He turned to the door. It opened automatically and he went through.

Cliff Dix remembered the room. In size, it could have doubled as a metro station. There was no office equipment in sight save two desks and neither of them looked especially like desks. Cliff had no idea what it might have cost to furnish this room. To buy the original paintings, to fill the shelves with their long rows of Morocco leather bound books, books that looked as though they had never been touched since they had been shelved originally. To purchase the undoubtedly hand-made heavy furniture. He wondered if the president's office in the White House was this elaborate.

Only one of the desks was occupied, and that by Walter Hardenberg, Director of the Inter-Continental Bureau of Investigation and Cliff's ultimate boss. Though he had only met the man that once before, and then in company with a score of other new agents, the face was well known.

Walter Hardenberg had held this position practically forever. He was now white-haired and gone to weight more than was usually evident when he was on Tri-Di lens. Cliff suspected him of wearing a girdle on such occasions. His face was tight and mean, and his air was that of a man who had been giving orders for the greater part of his life and had seldom, if ever, had them disobeyed. Cliff had never even heard of anyone reputed to like Walter Hardenberg. He wondered if the other was married.

Cliff Dix came to what amounted to attention before the desk and said, "Agent Clifford Dix, sir, reporting as ordered."

The other took him in thoroughly before saying, heavily, "You look young to be an IBI agent."

"Yes, sir." What in the hell could you say to that?

The director grunted. "Possibly, that's one of the

reasons the computers selected you. Sit down, Dix." He motioned with his head to a heavy leather chair.

Cliff sat and tried to project an appearance of intelligence. He hadn't the vaguest idea of why he was here but it must be fairly important for a simple agent to be brought before the Chief.

Hardenberg ran his eyes over him speculatively for a few moments before saying, "What do you know about the Subversive Party?"

Cliff looked at him blankly, cleared his throat and said, "The what?"

"This new Subversive Party, confound it."

"I've never heard of it, sir."

"Don't you listen to the Tri-Di news and commentators?"

"Usually, sir. But I've been down in the boondocks, in Florida, on my vacation." Cliff Dix wasn't the man to truckle to anyone. He added, "It had another week to go."

The other waggled a hand negatively. "We wanted to get a man on this immediately. Out of our whole organization, the computers selected you. I don't know why, but how can you argue with a computer?"

"Yes, sir."

"Your assignment is to go to Center City, where they evidently have their central headquarters, join the organization and rise as high as you can in their inner circles. It is an assignment that might last for weeks, months, or even years. It's a top secret matter. You will discuss it with no one and will report only to me. I'll have you issued a tight beam transceiver with a Priority One to my own communications. Your expense account will be unlimited. It's possible that to crack their innermost circles you will have to resort to bribery. Their Central Committee, or whatever they call it, is most likely composed of dedicated men. However, there's almost always some sort of chink. Even Talleyrand betrayed Napoleon."

"Well, yes sir. But... what is this Subversive Party?"

"We don't know."

Cliff ogled him.

Hardenberg said, obviously irritated, "There's practically nothing in the data banks on them. They have a banking account in the National Data Banks. It's suspiciously small. We can't understand this. They have a post office box in the Center City post office."

"Center City? Why not Greater Washington? Or San-San or one of the other bigger cities?"

The director shook his head and said, "Center City is supposedly the *average* city of the United States. That's where they base so many polls, that's where manufacturers test out so many products. It makes sense that they would use it as their base."

"Well, how big are they, so far?"

"We don't know. Confound it, Dix, that's why we're sending you in. We've got to know more about them."

Cliff Dix didn't truckle. He said, "Why me? I don't know anything about subversion."

"Because the computers selected you as our best agent for the job, confound it."

"Well, what does this outfit want to do?"

"Evidently, from the Letters to the Editor pages and from their news releases and from a few interviews they've had with news commentators, they want to overthrow the government."

"Holy Zoroaster! Let's just arrest them."

"On what charge?"

Cliff gaped at him. "You just said that they want to overthrow the government!"

"Unfortunately, there's no law against it."

Cliff was still gaping. "How do you mean, sir?"

"They want to vote themselves into power. There's no law against it. If they can talk a majority of the electorate into voting for them, they can do anything they want. God only knows what stupid cloddy thought that one up, Thomas Jefferson or James Madison, or whoever, but that's the American Constitution."

Cliff sank back into his seat.

The Chief said, somewhat musingly, "Actually, we haven't had a real radical movement in this country since the Wobblies, back before the First World War." He could evidently see by Cliff's expression that the agent had never heard of the Wobblies. "The I.W.W." he said. "The International Workers of the World. They started about 1905 with a program calling for One Big Union to take over the means of production and abolish capitalism. There was a political plank old Daniel DeLeon worked in calling for the forming of a working class party with which they could come to power legally. As a result of that legality, the government of the time, for the first few years, couldn't get at them."

Cliff said, "What happened?"

"The government infiltrated quite a few *agents provocateurs* and through their efforts were able to get the political planks and Daniel DeLeon along with them thrown out of the Wobbly constitution. Then they were vulnerable and by the time the World War ended they were crumbling. Some of their leaders, such as Big Bill Haywood, jumped bail when arrested and fled to Moscow. But we haven't had a real radical organization in the country since then, not one of any size."

"How about the Socialist Party, the Communists?"

Hardenberg shook his head. "The Socialist Party twice received almost a million votes, once under Debs, once under Norman Thomas. But it was never a radical party. It was reformist, something like the Labor Party in England, the Social Democrats in Germany. The Communists? They never got off the ground in America. They never got more than about 25,000 votes. Some of our politicians of the time made their reputations by supposedly fighting communism; Martin Dies, Nixon, Joe McCarthy. But it was all hot air; the commies were never a threat to the United States. Their program didn't make sense. It was an organization with its head in Russia and its ass over here."

"Yes, sir."

The Chief looked at him. "So your job is to infiltrate this new Subversive Party and find out all about it. If it's actually dangerous, then possibly your job will be to act the *agent provocateur*, as did our Department of Justice men with the Wobblies and in some manner maneuver them around so that we'll be in a position to prosecute them."

He wound it up. "I've assigned you an office, right here on this floor. For the next few days you'll find out everything possible on the Subversive Party and do a quick review of the other radical organizations in our history, even the small ones, such as the DeLeonist Socialist Labor Party and the Trotskyities. At the end of that period you should have some idea of what your cover will be in Center City and how you expect to operate. I'll see you again then and go over it with you."

It was a dismissal. Cliff Dix came to his feet.

The Chief was already checking out something on his desk screen. Without looking up, he said, "Miss Bennet, in the outer office, will take you to your quarters."

In the outer office, Cliff said to the girl at the first desk, "Miss Bennet?"

She said, indicating, "That's Ruth Bennet, over there."

Cliff went over there and said, "I'm Agent Dix. Mr. Hardenberg said you'd take me to my office."

She came to her feet, smiling, and led the way, he following along behind, admiring the sway of her... behind.

When she had left him in his small office, Cliff sank down into the swivel chair at the desk and looked at the library booster screen and the phone screen in dismay. This was *really* a new one.

In spite of the rather lengthy interview with his boss, he didn't have the vaguest idea of where to start. Practically all that he knew was the name of the organization and that its headquarters was in Center City.

He dialed the National Data Banks and requested all the information they had on the Subversive Party.

Hardenberg had been right. They had precious little. The organization had opened a banking account in the National Data Banks banking section with one hundred fifty pseudo-dollars and had rented a post office box at the Center City postoffice. Theoretically the data banks held all the information about everything and everybody that was available. *All* of it.

He thought about that for a moment, then said

into the screen, "Who deposited the one hundred and fifty pseudo-dollars for the Subversive Party account?"

"It was transferred from the accounts of Morris Malone, John Zieglar and Jeremiah Kleiser," the metallic voice answered.

"Who is eligible to make pseudo-dollar transfers from the account?" Cliff said.

"Morris Malone, John Zieglar and Jeremiah Kleiser," the voice told him.

Cliff switched off the set and leaned back in his chair for a moment. He said softly, "Oh, they are, eh? They're probably members of the Central Committee, or whatever it was the Chief called it."

He switched the screen back on and got the Universal Credit Card numbers of the three, and then said, "I want the Dossier Complete of Morris Malone."

The computer voice said, "Do you have the priority to request a citizen's Dossier Complete?"

"I am Agent Clifford Dix of the Inter-Continental Bureau of Investigation." He brought out his I.D. card and stuck it in the screen's slot.

And there, on the screen, was the life of Morris Malone. All vital statistics. His health record since childhood. His education. His military record— none. His crime record— practically none, a few traffic violations. His political affiliations— none. His marriage record— none.

Cliff went through it with care, occasionally making a note on a pad to the side of his screen with his stylo.

When he was through, he ordered the Dossier Complete of John Zieglar and perused that just as thoroughly, and then that of Jeremiah Kleiser.

When he was through, hours later, he switched off the screen and slumped back into his chair.

Three of the most average citizens in the country. All three on Guaranteed Annual Income. All three with at least averagely good educations. None with any crime record. None with any record of ever having worked at a paying job, though all had applied for them in their different fields. Only one with any military background... one hitch. None with any record of political activity, even to the point of having voted in a presidential or any other election. Not that that was any big deal, less than half the citizens eligible to vote bothered any more. The nearest thing to a crime record was John Zieglar's having been thrown into the drunk tank twice.

He thought about that and made a mental note of it. Hadn't one of the Old Bolsheviks, Bukharin, or one of the other top buddies of Lenin, been on the guzzle? And then when he got in trouble with Stalin, during the purges, he broke down and traded his soul for the vodka he needed. Yes, it might pay remembering that one of the top Subversive Party members couldn't control his drinking.

He switched the screen back on and said, "Transcribed News section. I want played back for me every news item and every commentator's reference to the Subversive Party."

The Tri-Di screen lit up and there before him was a news reporter scowling in bewilderment at a note he was holding in his hand.

Finally, the reporter looked up into lens and said, "Folks, here we have the latest press release of the new and aggressive Subversive Party, of whom I'm sure you've already heard. They are advocating the formation of an organization to be called The

Veterans of Future Wars, the VFW. They are of the opinion that young people, both male and female, should, upon reaching military age, receive pensions. They argue that the victims of future wars should have the right to enjoy their pensions *before* the war comes along and while they are still in good enough health to enjoy it. Later, they might be wounded, or even dead. Why should pensions go only to those who survive a war?" The reporter shook his head in bewilderment. He added, "The Subversive Party urges that if you are interested in the VFW, or in joining the SP, that you write to Post Office Box 1001, Center City."

Cliff Dix flicked off the set for the moment. "Holy Jumping Zoroaster," he said. "They'll get the vote of every pacifist in the country."

He flicked the set back on and there was one of the more prestigious news commentators there. He, too, looked a bit on the bewildered side.

But he said, "Ladies and gentlemen, I have decided to devote my today's fifteen minutes to a question brought up by the National Executive Committee of the Subversive Party."

So that was the real name of the central committee. Cliff made a note of it.

The commentator was saying, "The Subversive Party states that, if and when they come to power, all children physically able will be required to go to summer schools of their choice for two months each year. They must be open air, though the choice of seaside, mountains, lakes, forests will be up to the child. All expenses will be borne by the nation. The reasons for this step are three. First the National Executive Committee, in its first suggestion of levity I have seen, claims that it will take them, and I quote, 'out of the hair of adults.' Second, it will be good for their health. They'll be able to cough some of the smog, which they've been accumulating for the other ten months of the year, out of their lungs. Third, the schools will all be nudist, to get out of their systems all the nonsense that they have learned at home, or wherever, about modesty and such ridiculousness."

The commentator coughed and said, "Now let us take this up point by point. I will not argue about . . ."

Cliff switched him off.

"Zoroaster," he complained. "They'll wind up with the vote of every nudist in the country, not to speak of every health crackpot." He thought about it for a minute and added, "Not to speak of all the parents who hate their kids."

When he had finished listening to every Tri-Di newscast that had referred to the Subversive Party he turned to the newspapers and magazines. Largely, these accounts were in the form of letters to the editor and often signed by names that looked suspicious to him. However, there were some news items as well, though thus far the organization had never made the front pages.

The first item he read went:

SUBVERSIVE PARTY DEMANDS
RETURN OF TEXAS TO MEXICO

*Center City, August 3. The National Executive Committee of the newly-emerged Subversive Party declared today that if and when elected they will return Texas to the Mexicans and 'wipe out that blot upon our nation's history.'*

*Contending that the Alamo was garrisoned by United States volunteers, soldiers of fortune and adventurers, rather than by Texans, and that such men as Davy Crockett, Jim Bowie and William Travis were Americans rather than local patriots, the Subversive Party declared that even the flag flown over the fortress was that of a contingent of New Orleans volunteers.*

*A spokesman for the party stated that it is long past time that the wrong done Mexico be rectified.*

Cliff Dix blinked at the screen. "Holy smokes," he said, "that'll get them the vote of every *chicano* in the Southwest."

He scowled. "But then they'll lose the vote of every WASP in the state." He shook his head. "But for that matter no outfit called the Subversive Party would get the WASP vote in Texas anyway."

In sudden irritation, he put a call through to the editor of the paper.

When the other's face faded in on the phone screen, Cliff snapped, "See here, why in the world would you run a story on something as idiotic as the bunch of subversives advocating Texas be returned to the Mexicans?"

The other said patiently, "Listen, you should try and fill a newspaper these days. Would you rather read a report on the fact that the Chinese are building a new textile mill in Hangkow? Or would you like a blow by blow description of a second rate chess tournament in Buenos Aires? This Subversive Party comes up with something really new almost every day. And letters pour in from our readers. Some for, some against, but at least they're interesting."

Cliff sighed, switched the other off and returned to his task.

# 4

When Jed Kleiser entered the living room of Morris Malone's home it was to be confronted with a shambles. Most of the furniture had been moved out into other rooms. There were now three desks, each with a voco-typer upon it. There were several used steel files. Everywhere, against walls, in chairs, on the tops of the files, were stacked leaflets, brochures and stationery.

"Holy Zoroaster, this place is a mess," he said.

Morris looked up from a letter. "Hi, Comate," he said. "What spins?"

Jed looked at him, and said, "What in the hell's this Comate stuff?"

"It's our salutation," Morris told him. "What we call fellow members of the organization. I considered Comrade, but the commies loused that up. Brother sounds too religious. Colleague is too formal. How are you doing with the think tank bit?"

"I got three more double-domes. Professors from the Center City University City. You were right. Practically all of them get so excited they pee in their pants when they're invited to join a think tank."

"Don't they object to being affiliated with an organization with a name like the Subversive Party?"

Jed pushed a pile of leaflets aside on the couch so that he could sit down. "Naw," he said. "You couldn't knock that bunch of egg-heads if you wanted to. They'd join the Sadist and Masochist Party to get into a think tank."

"What are they thinking about?"

"Damned if I know."

"Did you collect their membership fees?"

"Sure. Deposited them in the National Data Banks. In fact, one of them ponied up a hundred pseudo-dollars donation, so I made him chairman of the think tank. How're you doing with the mail?"

"We've got twenty-eight requests for membership so far today. The new forms came from the printer this morning. I send each applicant one, with instructions on how to transfer five bucks from his pseudo-dollar account so that he can join up as a candidate member. There's a big hint for donations, too."

"Wizard," Jed said. "Where in the hell's Jack? Man, am I tired. I've been up half the night writing news releases and editors' columns."

Morris said, stretching wearily, "He's over at a jewelry manufacturer's, getting a kickback arrangement for gold rings and pins with our emblem. We'll recommend that all members wear them."

Jed said, "Emblem? I didn't know that we had an emblem."

"Sure. You've gotta have an emblem. A symbol for the Party. Jack and I dreamed one up. The commies had the crossed hammer and sickle, the Nazis had the swastika, the Democrats had the elephant and the Republicans had the jackass."

"Donkey," Jed said.

"From the last few presidents they fielded, I'll stick to my guns. Jackass."

"Well, what's our symbol?"

"The upraised forefinger. It won't be stated right out, but the implication is obvious. One of our prime slogans will be, *Screw you, Jack, I'm All Right.*"

Jed flinched. He said, "Wizard, but isn't that, ah, a little raw?"

"Hell, no. We want to make it clear to everybody that joins up that there's going to be something in it for him. He's not joining up because he's a do-gooder. He's out for himself. By the way, our first pamphlet, *Subversives of the World, Unite*!, will be delivered this afternoon. We've got it priced at one pseudo-dollar."

Jed said, "Wizard, but how in the hell did you pay the printer?"

"I stalled him," Morris said reasonably. "After reading the pamphlet himself he joined up. He knows a good thing when he sees it. We'll have him print our book, *Subversive Manifesto* when I get it finished. He's in on the ground floor, and knows it. I even got a fifty pseudo-dollar contribution from him. He'll make tens of thousands from us before he's through— we'll get various kickbacks, of course."

"Of course," Jed said unhappily. "But I thought that we were going to sell the book through one of the regular publishers."

Morris was indignant. "The hell with that. Why should we let them get into our gravy? We'll print it ourselves, put a price of ten pseudo-dollars on it and sell it through the mails. It'll be required reading for all party members, and we'll let anybody who wants to, buy it, of course. But no sales to libraries. Anybody who wants to read it has to pony up."

Jed said, "Something just occurred to me. We could have official stationery printed. The party emblem on it, and the paper a light suede in color.

Sell it to the membership, with the recommendation that all their correspondence be done on it."

The other made a note. "Good idea. We'll soak them twice what stationery usually costs."

Morris stretched again and came to his feet. He said, "Look, Jed, you take over. I'm bushed. I'm going to take a walk to loosen up my muscles. This thing's avalanching so fast we haven't got the manpower to take care of it."

"Sure, Mo," Jed said. "We're going to have to get some help around here. There's too much work for three men to do. Aren't there any mopsies here in Center City that have joined up?"

"Not so far," Morris said, heading for the door. "Besides, where'd we put 'em? We've got to rent some offices."

"Yeah," Jed said sourly. "When all three of us are in here, with the desks and the files and all this crud there's hardly room to turn around. But where'd we get the pseudo-dollars to rent offices?"

"Holy Zoroaster will provide," Morris told him, yawning mightily and heading for the door. "Those membership registrations are just beginning to roll in. Wait'll our new membership policy begins to snowball."

When he was gone, Jed slipped into the chair he had vacated, made a wry mouth, and picked up the letter on the top of the heap of those that hadn't as yet been opened.

It was an abusive crackpot missive, written by hand by someone who obviously hadn't gotten further than grammar school. Jed read the first paragraph and filed it in the wastebasket.

He took up the next letter. It was an application for membership from some character out in

California. He took up one of the membership application blanks, two of the Subversive Party leaflets and a brochure and stuffed them all in an envelope. He stuck the envelope in the voco-typer, took up the letter and read off the address. The typer ejected the envelope and he stuck it in the "Out" tray on the desk and reached for another letter.

He growled, "Hell, here I am on Guaranteed Annual Income and putting in more work than if I was holding down a job. And, so far, I haven't made a pseudo-dollar out of it." He grunted and added, "What I need is a union."

The identity screen on the door buzzed and he looked up. The face there was that of a stranger. Jed got up and activated it so that the other could see him as well.

The newcomer was a fresh faced, nice looking young man who looked somewhere in his early twenties.

Jed said, "What'd you want?"

"Mr. Morris Malone?"

"Comate Malone isn't here right now."

"I came to join the Subversive Party. I couldn't locate any headquarters, so I came here."

Jed opened up and the other entered. He was somewhat better dressed than citizens who had to subsist on GAI. Jed led the way back into the living room.

The other looked around.

Jed Kleiser said, "Have a seat." He motioned at the place on the couch where he had been seated himself before Morris had left. It was the only part of the couch not piled with Party leaflets.

The other sat down, frowning, and looked about the room again. He said, "It's a bit chaotic, isn't it?"

Jed said easily, "We've been having a little difficulty locating suitable headquarters." He added, "Some landlords are a bit leery about renting to an organization with a name like ours. But it won't be long. How did you get this address? The only one we've used, thus far, is a post office box."

The other crossed his legs and said, "I'm a private investigator. It was no big problem."

"Private investigator?"

"That's right. Private detective, private eye, shamus, and all that sort of curd. There aren't many of us any more. In fact, that's why I moved to Center City. There are none at all in business here. It's a tough racket these days but at least I'm not on GAI. I make a living."

Jed ran a hand over his lean face and said skeptically, "Well, why would you want to join the Subversive Party?"

The other said evenly, "Because I know a good thing when I see one. This is going to grow. Whether or not you ever come to power is another thing but at this stage of the game it's going to grow. I want in on the ground floor."

"Hmmm," Jed said. "Why do you think it's going to grow? And what ground floor? By the way, what's your name? I'm Jed Kleiser and I'm a member of the National Executive Committee."

"My name's Richard Oppenheimer," Cliff Dix said. "I've checked out every bit of information on the Subversive Party in the National Data Banks, including all news broadcasts and all media accounts in general. You've got a natural. In the past, minority parties would concentrate on one element or another. The working class, the tax payer, a racial group, pacifists, or whatever. And by doing so, they'd eliminate from their following all other groups. You've got a new slant. You're appealing to the whole minority field. Or, at least, all those that aren't diametrically opposite. After all, you can't be both pro Ku Klux Klan and Black. By the way, what's your stand on war? I didn't find anything in particular on that."

Jed said, "We're about to come out with a very strong stand on war. We're going to put the Army, Navy and Air Force in mothballs. All we're going to keep operative is enough atomic weapons to clobber anybody who gives us any trouble. So far as what little army remains, we're going to adopt the Italian strategy. If all armies conducted themselves like the Italian army, there wouldn't be any more wars."

"The Italian strategy?" Oppenheimer said, frowning.

"That's right. When they go into battle they all give the double fascist salute, both arms upraised. And their battle cry is, 'I surrender.' However, if, in spite of our efforts there *is* another war, we'll make it our policy to send in generals as the first wave of attack. They'll be our expendable shock troops. The second wave will be colonels and lieutenant-colonels. The third, majors. The fourth captains and lieutenants. If this doesn't do it, the non-coms go in. All privates remain in the rear, some twenty miles, observing the action with binoculars or on Tri-Di screens, if the battle is being covered by cameramen. During such battles, all privates are issued free beer and potato chips."

"Holy Jumping Zoroaster," the self-named Richard Oppenheimer blurted.

"Indeed. And now let's get back to this you wanting in on the ground floor fling."

"Just a minute," the other said. "How about the Navy?"

"Well, we'll make a new ruling. In the old days, the theory was that the captain go down with the ship. We'll change that so that all officers go down with the ship. We've got some other odds and ends about what remains of the military. They'll be required to do all their shopping in the Pxs. And all prices in a PX will be double."

Richard Oppenheimer shook his head in admiration. He said, "See? That's what I mean. You appeal to a score of different groups, not just one. You'll scoop up the pacifists wholesale."

"The ground floor, you mentioned," Jed said.

"Oh, yes. As I say, I know a good thing when I see one. This organization is in its infancy. It will grow. You'll need a good many officers, there'll be a good many jobs. My background is of value."

"How do you mean?"

Oppenheimer looked about the room. "Well, just for beginners, do you have, or know how to operate, a mop?"

Jed looked at him blankly. "A mop? Cleaning houses these days is automated."

"A mop, an electronic mop. How do you know that this room isn't being bugged by the Inter-Continental Bureau of Investigation?"

Jed looked about the room, his face still blank. "It never occurred to me."

The other said easily, "Well, these things occur to me. I'm in the profession. I'm well up on matters pertaining to the police, the IBI and so forth."

Jed said, "I see. And you want to join the Subversive Party and be of use as a member?"

"That's correct. I'm ambitious. I want to get on the Party payroll as soon as possible. And I've got the ability to work hard and rise in the ranks."

"Hmmm," Jed said. "I suspect that you're right. Okay, here's a membership blank. Make it out. Here's a National Data Bank banking section exchange transfer screen. Transfer five pseudo-dollars to the account of the Subversive Party. Your dues will be another five pseudo-dollars a month. I'll make out a Candidate Membership for you."

Jed looked down to a report on the desk top. "Your membership number will be 1082. That obviously is a low number. Low numbers are a prestige item in this organization. In the future, it'll be worth its weight in carats of diamonds. From our members with low membership numbers we'll largely select our officials, our leaders and so forth."

The other looked at him. "Number 1082? Is that all the membership you have?"

Jed smiled benignly. "This is Center City, our national headquarters. Members are being signed up locally all over the country."

Which was true . . . in a way. But Jed assumed the other would consider it in another way, which he evidently did. In actuality, the current membership was exactly eighty-five, including the three members of the Triumvirate.

The newcomer was making out the card with his stylo. He said, "What's this Candidate Member thing?"

Jed said smoothly, "It's a new Party policy. A newcomer cannot become a Full Member of the Subversive Party until he has recruited two other Candidate Members, who, in turn, contribute their membership fee."

Oppenheimer paused for a moment in his writing. He said, "The old chain letter bit."

"I beg your pardon?"

"It was a racket they had back in the 1930s or '40s. Never mind. What does a Full Member have that a Candidate Member doesn't?"

"He can hold office in the organization and can, ah, vote."

"How do you mean, *ah*, vote?"

"Basic Party decisions will be put to the vote of the organization as a whole. We're very democratic."

The younger man looked at him quizzically. "Who originates the decisions to be decided upon?"

Jed said virtuously, "The National Executive Committee, headed by the Triumvirate."

"Well, how did the National Executive Committee and the Triumvirate get to their position?"

Jed was still virtuous. "Democratically, of course. They were originally democratically elected by the entire membership." He didn't bother to mention that at the time the entire membership consisted of him and Mo and Jack, nor that the whole National Executive Committee also consisted of the same three.

Richard Oppenheimer finished the rest of his application, put his Universal Credit Card in the credit transfer slot and said, "Please transfer five pseudo-dollars from this account to that of the Subversive Party."

"Carried out," the computer voice said.

He looked up at Jed. "Wizard. Now, after I've gotten my two new Candidate Members how do I go about getting to become a member of the National Executive Committee? I told you I was ambitious."

Jed said smoothly, "Such positions are open only to Senior Party Members."

The new Candidate Member took him in for a long, empty moment. He said finally, almost as though in resignation, "How do you become a Senior Party Member?"

"The first requirement is that you have recruited at least five new Candidate Members. It also helps if you have shown your devotion to the organization by making donations, that sort of thing."

"I see." Oppenheimer thought about that for awhile then sighed and brought forth his Universal Credit Card again. He put it in the slot of the credit transfer device and said, "Please transfer five hundred pseudo-dollars from this account to that of the Subversive Party."

"Carried out," the computer voice said.

Jed was taken aback but he attempted not to show it. He would have liked to put over the impression that donations of that magnitude were every day affairs.

The other came to his feet, saying, "I'll get to work on the job of recruiting my two new Candidate Members so that my full membership will take effect. I've just moved to Center City so I don't know many people here. However, there are a couple of fellows back in Greater Washington I've already discussed the Party with. They were largely sympathetic. I think they'll come in."

"Wizard," Jed said.

"Do you have a branch in Greater Washington where they could join up?"

Jed was still playing it smooth. He said, "I'd have to check that. It's not my department." He handed the other two of the membership blanks, and some of the party leaflets. "However, it's no problem. They can sign up and transfer their five pseudo-dollars directly to our account in the National Data Banks."

"All right," Oppenheimer said. He turned to go

but at that time Jack Zieglar entered.

He wore a picturesque suede shirt, a double Sam Browne belt, of black leather, black riding pants, and suede boots that came half way to the knee.

At first, Jed closed his eyes in pain, but he said, "Comate Zieglar, this is our latest Candidate Member, Comate Robert Oppenheimer."

The two shook hands and sized each other up.

Jed said, "Jack is Commander in Chief of our Minute Men, our pseudo-military organization."

Robert Oppenheimer made a mental note of that while saying a few of the usual amenities, and then left. So they had a pseudo-military organization. Walter Hardenberg would undoubtedly be interested in that.

Jack looked after him.

Jed said, "I suspect that there goes our soon to be Gauleiter of Secret Police, or some other high ranking member of the outfit."

"Secret Police? What Secret Police?"

"He's a private investigator and knows all about electronic bugs, police matters and so forth. And he's all gung ho about climbing in Party ranks. He just donated five hundred pseudo-dollars."

Jack whistled softly. "He did, hey? But he's kind of young for a position like that, isn't he? And what do you mean, Secret Police?"

"Not if he's got the drive. Billy the Kid was only twenty-one when he got nailed. Octavius was nineteen when he took over the Roman Empire. Napoleon was still in his early twenties when he made his first big victories. How do I know about our secret police? We'll have to take it up with Mo."

Jack picked up the application blank Oppenehimer had just made out and went over to a library booster screen. He flicked it on and said, "I want the

Public Dossier of Richard Oppenheimer." He read off the identification number.

When the new member's available to the public dossier—as constrasting to a Dossier Complete—came onto the screen Jack Zieglar read it slowly. Then he turned back to his companion and said, "He's twenty-five years old, a private investigator, university degree, no crime record, no military service. Just recently moved here to Center City. Has an apartment in the Miller building upper reaches and an office in the lower."

"Wizard," Jed said. "He'll probably make a great member. Where in the hell did you get that outfit? What's this belts crossed across the chest bit?"

Jack beamed. "Great uniform, eh? I figured the crossed belts made it look more like a Minute Man."

"You look more like Pancho Villa to me," Jed said. "How'd you do with the jeweler?"

"Fine. He saw the possibilities immediately and even came up with another idea. Gold belt buckles with our emblem on them. He joined up himself and browbeat two of his staff into joining as Candidate Members, so he's already a Full Member. He gave me a thousand dollar advance toward our kickback."

"Did you deposit it to our account?"

"Sure."

"Well, we can use it." Jed looked around the room. "We've simply got to get out of here and into a suite of presentable offices. We've got to have some place people can come and not get the impression that we're a bunch of cheap cloddies. That Oppenheimer kid looked doubtful when he first saw our set-up."

"I don't know why I get a funny feeling about him," Jack said, looking at the door through which the younger man had passed a few minutes before.

# 5

Morris Malone strode along the sidewalk, trying to exercise away his tension. He felt as though he had been sitting in that cluttered living room for months. In actuality, the Triumvirate *was* putting in endless hours of their time. Somehow, they were going to have to delegate some of their duties.

He tried to take his mind off the new party, but couldn't.

They had gotten themselves into a hole. New members were coming in, increasingly fast, with that new brainstorm of Jed's, the Candidate Member who didn't become a Full Member until he produced two new recruits, or a Senior Member until he had recruited five more. But the thing was, so far they hadn't been able to harness the activities of these new members. They didn't even have a headquarters here in Center City, not to speak of anywhere else in the country. Somehow, they had to get going. They had to rent some halls, give some speeches, start up a national official newspaper or magazine, begin to make sounds as though they were going to contest some elections.

Somebody said, "Cheers, Mo. What spins?"

He hadn't seen her approaching.

Morris Malone had known Karen Landy vaguely for years. She was a strikingly handsome, seemingly well adjusted young woman. If Morris resembled the early Henry Fonda, she, in turn, resembled the early Ava Gardner. She was a red head, her figure was a bit spare, but she projected herself in such a way that she was seldom in a room with other women that she didn't dominate. She was handsome, she was alive, she was earnest.

Morris Malone wasn't going any place in particular, he was just exercising. He fell into step beside her, though she had been walking more briskly than he had. He'd been strolling.

He said, "Cheers, Karen. How's the last of the lady libbers these days?"

"Women's lib, not ladies'," she said definitely.

"What's the difference?"

"The term lady is almost invariably used as a genteelism."

"Wizard," he grinned at her. "What's a genteelism?"

She thought for a moment, then said, "Suppose somebody says, 'The swimmer was too far out to make it back to the beach, so she went to the bathroom in the ocean.'"

That brought a chuckle from him.

She ignored the laugh and said, "Now, obviously, she didn't go to the bathroom while swimming in the ocean. She urinated, or, if you will, took a leak, but there are no bathrooms in the ocean— at least, not that I know of."

"What's that got to do with ladies?"

"All female humans are women, but few are ladies. It's another genteelism. A lady, by definition, is a British aristocrat, or, stretching it, a woman of gentility and discrimination. Ladies of the evening, so called, are women but they're not ladies. They're whores. All ladies are women, but all women are not ladies. Just as all men are not gentlemen."

Morris was laughing. "All right," he said. "I surrender. But how's women's lib getting along?"

She said bitterly, "It's folding up. Evidently, we've been libbed to the point that most of the militants have dropped away."

"Oh?" he said. "The goals have been reached?"

"In a way. We were fighting for equal pay with men. We've pretty much gotten it. But the thing is, practically nobody works any more. Practically everybody's on GAI. Then take housekeeping. It's automated. You can't demand of a man that he share housekeeping, when you don't do any of it either—or so little that it doesn't make any difference. Child raising? Anybody who doesn't enjoy raising kids can put them into child centers."

She scrutinized him, seemingly as though she had never really taken him in completely before. "You on GAI?" she said, challenge in her voice.

"Yeah," he told her. "But it's not my fault. I put in eight years studying to be a teacher. And now teaching is almost entirely automated. You?"

"No, damn it. I refuse to be a charity case, no matter that they call it by another genteelism, Guaranteed Annual Income. I'm a secretary. I make precious little more than if I was on GAI but at least I can hold my head up."

"A secretary?" he said, wheels beginning to turn.

"That's right. I'm the best damned secretary in Center City, and I'm not kidding. Of course," she added ruefully, "I'm one of the few secretaries left in Center City. My work, too, is rapidly being automated out from under me."

"Hmmmm," Morris said. "Listen, Karen, what do you say we drop into a bar and have a quick one and talk a little?"

She eyed him. "Talk about what?"

"The Subversive Party."

"What about it? I've heard a few items on Tri-Di about it. Sounds like a bunch of crackpots to me. They want to give Montana and Wyoming back to the Sioux and Blackfeet."

"And the buffalo," Morris said. "Also, Florida back to the Seminoles. Bulldozer down all those claptrap houses, motels, service stations and hamburger drive-ins."

She said, "Listen, Mo, are you a member?"

"One of the founders."

"Listen, to hell with going to a bar. We're only half a block from my house. Let's go over there."

"My arm twists easily," Morris told her, making his voice very earnest. "Very easily."

The home of Karen Landy was a far cry from that of Morris Malone, though it was similar in size and little more expensively furnished. But Karen was a lover of the arts and her taste was impeccable.

Dominating one wall was a Monet. Morris stared. He said, "Where in the hell did you get that? It's not a copy or a print."

Her eyebrows went up. "I'm surprised that you knew. It was left to me by my grandfather."

"Why don't you sell it and live off what you get for the rest of your life?"

"Would you sell your soul?" she said, throwing her bag to an empty chair, after extracting her Universal Credit Card from it. She headed for the autobar.

"I don't have one," he told her, sinking into a chair,

and, his voice more lemonish, "nor a Monet."

She said, "What'll you have? I'm having a pseudo-whiskey."

"Beer," he said. "I can't go that imitation guzzle. Which reminds me. That's an item that we'll have to put into the program. When we Subversives come to power we'll have to close down all distilleries and breweries."

"Holy Jumping Zoroaster," she said. "You'd lose the vote of every lush in the country." She returned with the drinks.

He took the glass she proffered. "No," he said, "we'd gain them. We'd inform all distilleries and brewers that they couldn't open again until they came up with really acceptable guzzle. Put taste back into spirits, put hops, body and strength back into beer. We Americans drink the worst beer in the world, always excepting the British, of course."

She took a chair across from him. "All right," she said. "All I know about the Subversive Party is a few items I picked up on Tri-Di. Tell me about it."

He told her in detail the program as it presently stood.

Once she got up to refresh their glasses. Two or three times she interrupted him to ask questions, but mostly she kept mum. At the end, she sat there for a long time before speaking.

Then she said, "Where do you stand on sex?"

"Sex?"

"Sex."

"I'm all in favor of it."

"Silly. I mean how does the Subversive Party stand on the question?"

"Well," Morris said unhappily. "That subject hasn't come up as yet. That's one of the reasons I'd like to see an old hand women's libber such as yourself in the upper ranks of the organization. Any suggestions?"

"Ummm. I've got a pile of them. I've been in revolt on matters sexual since I was in my early teens and couldn't get satisfactorily laid because I was jail bait. The only sex I had was in places like the back seats of hovercars with gawky kids who didn't really know how to perform."

Morris cleared his throat and said cautiously, "What changes did you have in mind?"

Karen went into her ideas with a vengeance. "I feel that at the age of fifteen every girl should be required to appear before a government doctor for an examination. If she's still a virgin, her hymen will be surgically removed and then she'll be given one of these new birth control shots that last for a year. If she's not a virgin, she'll just be given the shot."

Her visitor said, "Go on. What happens to the virgin?"

She finished her drink. "She'll be required to take on a sex instructor, of her choice, for sex education."

"Uh, what kind of sex education?"

She looked at him scornfully. "What do you think?"

"Well, where'll you get the instructors?"

"Don't be silly. Volunteers, of course. The country's full of eligible men who go for young girls. We'll screen them carefully, needless to say. Only the best types, both physically and mentally."

"What happens to boys when they reach the same age?"

"Substantially the same thing. If at the age of fifteen they're not getting all the nooky they want, they'll be assigned a female sex instructress who'll take over their sex education and fill their normal requirements."

"Wouldn't you have a little more trouble getting women volunteers than men?"

"I wouldn't think so. Not when it's presented as a community duty and absolutely accepted morally. Besides, one woman could take care of several pupils, where most men can only go so many times. It would deal a death blow to masturbation."

Morris Malone tried to inject a light note. "Is that necessarily a good idea? Wasn't it Benjamin Franklin who said, 'Masturbation is its own reward.'?"

She got up and went over and got them a third drink apiece and returned with them.

She said, "That's only a little funny. To go on, every year the girl will have to show up again for another antipregnancy shot."

In protest, Morris said, "Where will the new babies come from?"

"Later in life. Today, most girls become pregnant before they should. It's not good for their health and, besides, they're not adult enough to be trusted to raise our children. We'll rule that no woman can have a child until twenty-one, soonest. Then, if she wants one, she can apply to the Genetics Bureau."

"Married or not?"

"Of course, married or not. If somebody wants to get married, let 'em. But if they don't want to, it has nothing to do with having children. And we'll adopt the Moslem method of divorce. All either of the married couple have to do is say, 'I divorce thee,' three times and they're divorced. And no alimony or child support, either. The parent who takes the kid gets its Guaranteed Annual Income until it's eighteen. Then the child gets it."

Morris took a pull at his beer. He said, "Wow. I thought the ideas Jed and Jack and I had were on the far out side."

Karen pursued it. "To get back to this matter of her applying to have a child. If she does, she's given a thorough genetic examination. So is the man she wishes to be the father. If they're both suitable, they're allowed to go ahead."

"Hold up there, a minute," Morris protested. "Suppose she picks a man to be the father who isn't interested in her? Maybe he's married to somebody else, or doesn't like her."

"If he's suitable otherwise, he'll have to be the father, through artificial insemination, if nothing else. Of course, in such cases he'd have no obligations to the child. By keeping a close rein on this, we'll lick both the population explosion and upbreed the race. Survival of the fittest, that's the slogan we'll bring back. We're going to stop breeding idiots and cripples. If deformities come along, the attending doctor will bash them over the head, or some such. We don't want them growing up, breeding, and passing on their genes."

Morris winced. He said, "Won't a howl go up from some of the do-gooders?"

"What do you mean, do-gooders? *We're* the do-gooders. Anybody who howls at a measure as important as that should be shot."

"It seems to me that we'd wind up shooting a lot of people."

"Only jerks, though the Holy Zoroaster knows the country's full of them. But it'd help stonewall the population explosion."

Morris Malone said cautiously, "You keep saying *we*. Does that mean you're in?"

"You're damn right I'm in. What you need is a woman's auxiliary. Have you got any women members as yet?"

"A few, scattered around the country."

"Wizard," Karen said definitely. "What can you afford to pay me? Obviously, it's a full time job. Besides, you've already told me that your basic slogan is *What's In It For Me?*"

Morris Malone blinked at her. "All the rest of us are on Guaranteed Annual Income. Couldn't you quit your present job and go onto GAI for the time being?"

"Hell, no. I told you that I refuse to become a charity case."

Her guest sighed. "What're you making now?"

"A hundred fifty pseudo-dollars a week."

"All right. We'll up it to one hundred seventy-five. In a few weeks, the treasury ought to be on its feet. Report for duty in the morning at my home. You're a professional secretary. Wizard. We can use one."

"Okay. How do I go about becoming a member?"

"You will make out a registration blank and transfer five pseudo-dollars to the organization. That makes you a Candidate Member. Then you line up two more members and that makes you a Full Member. Then you line up five more Candidate Members, and that makes you a Senior Member and you're eligible to hold down Party offices, even up to the National Executive Committee, to which you'll undoubtedly belong as head of the Women's Auxiliary."

She looked at him for a long doubtful moment. "I've got to go through all that routine?"

And he said, oozing unction, "All the other members of the National Executive Committee have. I don't think it would be a good idea to start a precedent."

She thought about it. "I've got two friends who'd come in. Former women's libbers too. In fact, I'm beginning to suspect we'll be able to corral just about every member of the women's lib organization I used to belong to."

She yawned and said, "It's beginning to get a little late. Suppose we go out into the kitchenette and whip up something to eat."

"Whip up something to eat? Do you mean that you do your own cooking, rather than just dialing your meals from the community kitchens?"

"Damn well told," she said. "And when I'm on the Executive Committee I'm going to have a few words to say about the Party program on the arts— and, among the arts is cooking."

She stood and headed for the kitchen. "But right now let's get something onto our stomachs and then get to bed."

He gaped at her a little, at first, but then came to his feet and followed.

# 6

Morris Malone sat at the small table in the kitchenette while Karen efficiently whipped together a meal. She'd put an apron over her tailored slacks and he made no effort to keep his eyes from her bottom as she stirred a dish, bent over to check the oven from time to time, that sort of thing. She had a more ample bottom than he had formerly thought.

He said, "What else about the relationship between the sexes?"

Without turning from her work, she said, "Well, for one thing, if we're going to continue marriage at all, I think we ought to legalize both polygamy and polyandry."

"Both?"

"Both."

"Well, why?"

She turned and gestured at him with her tasting spoon. "The trouble with marriage today is monogamy. It's not natural. Men never have abided by it. They always had their mistresses, when they could afford them, or their occasional rolls in the hay, whenever they could get them. They kept a stricter rein on women but even then, in spite of laws, religious taboos, and the so-called moral code, there was one hell of a lot of cheating going on. It led to most of the bad feeling in a marriage. Husbands and wives, both, were continually accusing each other of cheating. Given polyandry and polygamy and everybody could spread their sex around as far as they wanted."

Morris Malone shook his head and said, "Frankly, I don't even want to be married to one woman, not to speak of maintaining a harem."

"Well, you've got good sense, and I, frankly, feel the same way. But anyone silly enough to want to have half a dozen or so spouses, let 'em."

She brought a couple of dishes over and set the table.

He said, doubtfully, "Do you think your Woman's Auxiliary would go for that? I can see where possibly a lot of men would."

"Sure they would. In the old days, men used to be the providers and women were in a position to have to bow down to them, but that doesn't apply any more, even now, what with GAI and legal equality of the sexes, we're beginning to sample around in our sex lives. By the way, Women's Auxiliary isn't any good as a name. It sounds as though we're second class members of the Party. How about just calling us Subversivettes? We'll have a cute uniform, but otherwise we'll just be the same as men Party members, except that we'll concentrate on making women converts and specialize in angles pertaining to women."

"Cute uniform?"

She brought over the casserole she had prepared and sat down across from him and began to serve.

"Uummm. Very important that we have a really chic uniform designed for the Subversivettes. I read once about the WAVES and the WACS during the Second World War, the Navy and Army auxiliaries.

Recruiters for the army couldn't figure out why it was that the navy was getting several times as many women volunteers. It turned out that the women didn't like the kind of hats the WACS wore. So we'll get a really snappy outfit for us to wear in parades, at rallies and so forth, and half the women in the country will want to join up, just so they can wear one."

Morris shook his head in despair and tasted his food. "Hey," he said. "This is good. In fact, it's wizard."

"That's what I keep telling you. Cooking's an art. We've got to revive all of the arts. All out."

"We have?"

"Yes. It's the only thing that makes sense, Mo. All down through history the human race has been working like bastards just to produce enough food, clothing and shelter for everybody. Only a few weren't pushed by this pressure, the ruling classes. Only they had the leisure time to develop themselves culturally, to study and appreciate the arts. But now practically everybody has leisure. And what do they do? They sit in front of their Tri-Di sets and take trank pills, or drink beer."

"So, how can we change it?"

She pointed her fork at him. "It'll take awhile. We start with the kids. We give them every opportunity to find the art, or arts, in which the potentially excel. Painting, music, writing, handicrafts, whatever. They'll be tested continually and encouraged to develop in whatever particular field they tend toward."

"All kids aren't potential artists."

She was scornful of that opinion. "Why not? I don't claim that they're all potential *great* artists, or even great handicraft workers. But any normal human being can be taught some musical instrument, or to draw, to sculpture, or possibly to write. Certainly to the point where he or she will appreciate the arts more."

He thought about it while they finished the meal.

Afterwards she stood and picked up the dishes. "You can dry," she said.

He looked at her. "Dry what?"

"The dishes, silly."

"Why not just throw them into the disposal chute?"

"You obviously were so caught up in our conversation that you didn't notice what you were eating off of. This isn't the cheap plastic curd used by the community kitchens. Ceramics is an art too. I refuse to have less than beautiful things in my home."

Morris contemplated her. He said, "You know, I think that you're going to make one hell of an asset for the organization."

The dishes finished, Morris followed her back into the living room.

She said, matter-of-factly, even as she began to unbutton her blouse, "The bedroom's over here."

He swallowed and said, "Just a minute. I better call in to the boys and report. Supposedly, I was just out for a walk."

He went over to the phone screen and dialed his own house. Jack's face faded in.

Morris closed his eyes in suffering. "Where'd you get that shirt?"

Jack beamed. "Pretty nifty, eh? This is the new Minute Man shirt."

Morris said, "All right. Listen, I'm recruiting a new women's auxiliary— the easy way. I won't be in for awhile. Lock up, when you leave."

"Okay, Mo," Jack said. "The jeweler ponied up a thousand pseudo-dollars advance on our rake-off with him, and joined up, along with two of his employees. And another new recruit donated five hundred. In the evening mail, there were sixty-five new requests for membership. This thing is beginning to avalanche, Mo."

"Good. I just hired a secretary. She's also head of the Subversivettes, our new women's auxiliary. It sounds as though there's enough credit in the kitty to rent a suite of offices tomorrow. We'll get to it."

"Right. Who's the new secretary?"

"Karen Landy."

"Wizard," Jack said. "She's a good lay." His face faded.

"I'll soon find out," Morris Malone muttered.

He followed Karen into the bedroom. She had already stripped and now turned to face him.

"All right?" she smiled.

She looked even better out of clothes than she had in them. He didn't know how he had ever thought that she was less than averagely endowed. He began to tear off his own clothing.

She took up a coin from the night table next to the bed. It was an old fashioned coin from the days before the establishment of the pseudo-dollar.

She said, "I'll match you for who's the aggressor. Heads or tails?"

He looked at her blankly, even while getting out of his trousers. "What do you mean, heads or tails? You mean a sixty-nine, or straight?"

"No, silly. I mean, what do you take, when I flip the coin, heads or tails?"

"Oh, well, heads."

She flipped it so that it spun high and then landed on the bedspread.

"Tails," she said with satisfaction. "I'm the aggressor."

She peeled the bedspread back— Malone noticed that it was a beautiful handworked quilt of a type he hadn't seen outside a museum since he was a child— and climbed in, and looked up at him expectantly.

He came over, rather with care, and eyed her suspiciously. "How do you mean, the aggressor?"

"Get in," she said.

He got in beside her and began to reach for her.

"Just a minute," she said. "In the old days, especially on the first go, it was always the man who was the aggressor, who took the initiative. The woman was expected to play it coy. He'd start off by kissing her, and she'd be reluctant. Then he'd possibly feel her breasts, and she'd either protest or pretend she didn't know what he was doing. Then he'd run a hand up under her skirt, not very far at first, and she'd protest some more or pretend to push his hand away. After a bit of wrestling, she pretending modesty, he'd get her panties off. By this time, it was obvious what was going to happen. Exactly what she had figured on happening from the beginning, and exactly what he had hoped was going to happen. Nine times out of ten, he'd wind up on top of her— in the old missionary position, even though he might be twice her size and weight—pounding away. If the girl had an orgasm, she was lucky. But, of course, he always had one."

Morris Malone said suspiciously, "So those were the old days. I recall them as the good old days. Now, what happens in the new days?"

She held her hand up, fingers spread, the thumb

on top. She flipped the hand over, so her little finger was on top.

"Like that," she said. "We reverse the roles."

"Oh, oh," he said.

She bent over him, expertly.

He muttered, "I'm beginning to suspect that you've flipped that coin before. Can you make it come up whatever you want every time?"

"No," she murmured, her voice sultry. "Only about four out of five. My, you're already huge."

About midnight, she got up and trotted from the room. He looked after her. Her pink girlish bottom was memorable.

In five minutes she returned with two huge sandwiches and two plastics of cold beer.

"Man, this is service," he said.

"Don't get any crumbs in the bed," she told him, climbing back in.

They munched for awhile and then she said, "I've got another idea dealing with sex that we ought to advocate."

"Oh? What?"

"Venereal disease."

He stared over at her. "Advocate venereal disease? That's getting a little *too* damned subversive."

"Don't be silly. I mean cure it for all time." She took a swig of her beer.

"A nice trick if you could pull it off, but it seems to me that VD has been kicking around for a long time."

"Ummm. Back at the time of the Second World War they came up with the sulfa drugs and for a while sulfa would knock gonorrhea within a day or so, and I think maybe even syphlis. At least some cases of it. But after a while the germs that survived bred new strains that were resistant to sulfa. So then somebody invented penicillin and for awhile it would knock both venereal diseases."

"But the bugs adapted to that too," Morris said, finishing off his sandwich.

"Right. So they came out with a new antibiotic."

"And they adapted to that, too. And the germs have every intention of continuing to do the same. What's your big scheme?"

"We wait until the double-domes come up with a new antibiotic. We don't use it, hit and miss, like with the sulfas and penicillin. We don't give the bugs the chance to adapt to it. Within a period of twenty-four hours we inject every man, woman and child in the country with the new antibiotic. And I mean *everybody*. The president, all the congressmen, every bishop, every little old lady, every babe in arms, every invalid, every doctor— everybody."

He was ogling her. "You know," he said. "I think that it'd work."

"Sure it would work," she said in satisfaction. "Then what we'd do is post a medico at every point of entry to the country. Anybody wanting to enter the United States of America would have to submit to taking a shot of the new antibiotic; tourists, immigrants, diplomatic corps, everybody. Hell, if the Pope came over to visit the White House, we'd give him a shot. If the Queen came, she'd get it."

"I'll be damned," he said. "I'll have to work this into the *Subversive Manifesto*."

# 7

Jack Zieglar awoke from no deep dream of peace. He had hung one on the night before. He hadn't expected to but the continual pressure of all the unaccustomed work he was doing for the Party had piled up and instead of knocking it off after he'd had two or three to relax on he'd had two or three more. And then two or three more. And then . . .

Before opening his eyes he tried to remember where he was. Sometimes when he went on a tear he'd wake up in the morning in the damnedest places. When the fog rolled in, just about anything could happen to him, and usually did.

He opened one eye, suspiciously, but he was in his own bed in his own house. He wondered how he had ever made it. He opened the other eye and looked at the pillow next to him. There wasn't anyone there. If some mopsy had brought him home, she hadn't stayed. Thank heavens. He couldn't have performed this morning with a girl, feeling the way he did, if it had been the very latest Tri-Di sex symbol.

He pushed the covers down and cautiously got out of bed. To his surprise, his head stayed on. He made a beeline for the bathroom, showered and used depilatory on his face. He dressed in his new uniform, admired himself sourly in the mirror, and then forced himself into the kitchenette to dial breakfast. He wanted breakfast about as much as he wanted a broken ass, but he had long since found that there was exactly one way to get over a hangover. You got two hot meals under your belt, two hot meals that you were able to keep down. Then you were sober, the hangover gone— and you could start all over again.

Breakfast precariously secured, he took out his transceiver and dialed the time. He whistled. He hadn't known it was this late. Mo and Jed would give him a hard time. There was enough work for a score.

When he approached the Malone cottage it was to find an autohover truck parked before it. Jed came staggering out of the door with a large carton of leaflets in his arms. He put it in the back of the truck and looked at Jack accusingly.

"Where the hell have you been?" he said accusingly. "You look like the wrath of Holy Jumping Zoroaster."

"I've been hanging over," Jack told him. "What's going on here?"

"Mo rented a suite of offices. We're moving over."

Karen Landy emerged from the house with a smaller carton of brochures, followed by Morris Malone with a larger one.

Jed said to Jack Zieglar, "Come on. We'll get one of the steel files. Do you know Karen Landy? She's our new secretary and head of the Subversivettes, our woman's auxiliary."

"Cheers, Karen," Jack said to her. "What spins?"

"By the looks of you, your head," she said tartly, putting her load in the back of the truck. "What the devil kind of an outfit is that?"

"It's my Minute Man uniform," he said proudly.

"We're the Suede Shirts. I'm the Commander-in-Chief."

She shook her head, but said, "Suede, eh? I've got a friend who belonged to the same women's lib outfit I did. I think I can recruit her. She used to be a dress designer before the textile industry became so automated. She can design a suede uniform-dress, complete with a suede shoulder bag."

"That sounds good," Mo said, pushing his own carton into the truck. "And we can arrange for a kickback from the dress manufacturers and also one from the pocketbook people."

Jed and Jack Zieglar had gone back into the house for another load.

"Kickback?" Karen said, frowning.

"Sure kickback," Morris Malone said. "I keep telling you, we're all in this organization for what we can get out of it. Why should we let some manufacturer make all the profit? We'll nick them for plenty. Nothing happens in this party that doesn't somehow make a pseudo-dollar for us."

A stranger was strolling up the street, hands nonchalantly in pockets. He stopped before Morris and brought the right hand out and extended it and said, "Comate Malone?"

Morris shook but said, "Comate?"

"That's right. My name's Richard Oppenheimer. I became a Candidate Member yesterday and a Full Member today."

Morris took him in. "Already?" he said. "You mean you've got two new recruits already?"

"That's right. Couple of friends in Greater Washington. We'd already discussed the organization before I moved here to Center City. I got them on the phone and gave them the story. They were all gung ho to join. They've already ponied up their five pseudo-dollars." The newcomer looked at Karen Landy, who was taking him in speculatively, somewhat in the manner that men are supposed to undress a girl with their eyes.

Morris said, "Let me introduce Karen Landy, head of our Subversivettes."

"Call me Dick," Oppenheimer said, shaking, and noting that she shook hands like a man. "Can I help out here?"

"Sure," Morris said, heading back for the house. "We're moving to our new headquarters."

They were able to take all of the belongings of the organization in one load. All piled into the vehicle and Jed dialed it to the basement of the office building where they had rented their space. They unloaded the things into a freight elevator and went up to the tenth floor.

Jack said, "How much room do we have?"

Morris and Karen were the only two who had seen it thus far. Morris said, "Small reception room. Three offices. A conference room, some storage space and a rest room."

"Rest room," Karen said in an undertone of contempt. "A genteelism. A toilet, a John, you mean. How much rest do you get in a toilet?"

"Well, sometimes it can be pretty restful," Morris said mildly. "Come on, everybody, let's start getting this stuff inside."

When they had finished Jack Zieglar looked about appreciatively and whistled admiration. "Even furnished," he said. "How long are we going to be able to afford this set up?"

Jed said, "The way the treasury is, about two months. By that time, knock on wood, we can pray that more pseudo-dollars have come in. I wonder if we have any sign painters in the organization who could do signs on the doors."

Morris Malone said, "Let's all go into the conference room and have our first conference. There's an autobar in there and enough chairs for all of us."

They took seats around the heavy table. Jack went over to the autobar and called for orders.

"Deduct the bill from the account of the Subversive Party," Morris said grandly.

When the drinks were all served, he said, "The meeting of the National Executive Committee will come to order. Comate Landy, you can take notes, if any are needed and they probably aren't."

"Just a minute," Dick Oppenheimer said. He came to his feet and brought a metal gadget from an inner pocket. It looked something like an old fashioned fountain pen. He pressed a stud and then began going around the room, pointing the gismo here, there, everywhere, and particularly at any electronic equipment.

"What in the hell's that?" Morris Malone said to him.

"An electronic mop. I'm checking to see if this room's bugged."

They stared at him.

"Clean," Oppenheimer said finally, returning to his leather chair. "Now, what's this about the National Executive Committee coming to order? I'm not a member of the National Executive Committee. I'm not even a Senior Member as yet. I haven't gotten my five additional Candidate Members."

"We'll waive that temporarily," Morris said, "particularly in view of the fact that you undoubtedly shortly will have them. We like your style, particularly the speed with which you got your two new Candidate Members. And Jed told me about you donating the five hundred. We've already considered making you our National Organizer. Have you done any public speaking?"

"I was on the debating team at the university," Oppenheimer said. He was wary. "What's a National Organizer?"

Jed said, "Applications for membership are coming in like crazy. We're going to have to start local branches in all the big towns. Mo and I talked it over last night. Each branch will have a minimum membership of five. Later, we'll up that. Each branch will have a Senior Member branch organizer, a secretary and a propaganda committee."

"What's a propaganda committee?" Karen said. "I thought propaganda meant lies."

"Well, it doesn't," Jed told her. "It just means you're propogating your message, whatever it might be. It *can* be lies, but it doesn't have to be."

He looked at Dick Oppenheimer. "You'll go from town to town, where we've already signed up a minimum of five and organize them into a branch. You'll give pep lectures, try to get free Tri-Di time, recruit more members, put them to work distributing our leaflets, selling our pamphlets. Later, when we get the *Subversive Manifesto* into print, they can sell that too." He looked thoughtful. "We only have one pamphlet out so far but more are on the way. We'll sell them *Subversives of the World Unite* at a discount, say seventy-five cents a copy, and they'll make a little on each sale."

Jack protested that. "Then we'll only be making about fifty cents a copy. It costs a quarter to print."

"We can't hold onto all of it," Morris said.

Dick Oppenheimer said, "Now wait a minute. How do I finance this tripping around the country? What am I paid?"

Jed beamed at him. "We'll issue you two hundred pseudo-dollars a week, and expenses, but we expect you to pay for yourself very shortly with new applications for membership, collections at your hall meetings, and other donations. Everything you take in, of course, you deposit to our account in the National Data Banks. Later on, we'll probably put other National Organizers on the road, but you're the beginning, and if you make out you'll be First National Organizer, with all the others under you, and you'll get more pay. Okay?"

"Wizard," Dick Oppenheimer said. "I'm in. Give me the membership lists of the towns where we have more than five members and I'll start out tomorrow."

Morris said, "Any more matters to bring before the National Executive Committee?"

Jed looked over at Jack Zieglar, sitting there in his garish uniform.

He said, "I've been wondering about this Minute Man organization, our so-called Suede Shirts. How do we stand on racial questions?"

"We should be all for them," Morris said definitely. "We'll have a foreign federation for every race from the Australian Aborigines to the Zulus. Every race will have its own auxiliary."

Karen looked at him skeptically. "What will we promise them? Why should they want to join up?"

"We'll promise them everything. Remember, the basic reason for people joining the Subversive Party is that they think they'll get something out of it. We'll promise every Greek a government loan with which to open a restaurant. We'll promise every Indian tribe still remaining, all their former lands swiped by the white man. We've already promised the Mexicans to give Texas back to them. We'll promise the Italians free passage for all their relatives that want to come over here from the old country. Every Italian in Italy, especially Sicily, wants to come to America."

"Holy Zoroaster," Jack blurted. "How'll we ever deliver?"

"Don't be ridiculous," the other told him. "Who ever heard of a politician delivering? Once we're in, we'll tell them it was all campaign oratory."

Morris Malone carried it on. "Politicians never keep their promises. Did you ever read about Franklin D. Roosevelt? Before the United States got into the Second War, he said, 'Again and again I tell you I will not send your sons abroad to fight.' At the same time, he was doing such provocative little goodies as sending the Flying Tigers to fight against the Japanese in China, armed with the latest American planes, giving the British fifty destroyers to fight the U-Boats, arming American merchantmen and ordering American warships to shoot first if they saw a sub. He was also the president who made his first campaign on a tight budget platform. As soon as he got into the White House he began spending money like water.

"They're a bunch of crooks," he went on. "All politicians. Politics are so crooked that you have to be a crook to get anywhere in them. Take Tom Dewey. He made his name prosecuting the Mafia head, Lucky Luciano; got him sentenced to life, or something. And then, during the Second War, when Dewey was governor of New York, pardoned him. Why? It was unrealistic to keep him in prison, he said. Supposedly, it came out later, the reason Luciano was pardoned was so that the Mafia in Sicily would collaborate with the United States military."

Jack said, after another satisfactory pull on his second drink, "Well, anything else on this race question? I think Mo ought to work it into the *Subversive Manifesto*."

"What's this *Subversive Manifesto*?" Dick said.

"All radical parties have to have a manifesto," Jed told him reasonably. "Anybody knows that."

Morris said reflectively, "Maybe, after we come to power, we'll allow a few pogroms against the inferior races."

Karen ogled him. "Pogroms, inferior races? What inferior races? I thought you said we were going to have auxiliaries among all races."

"Oh, you know. Like Southerners and New Yorkers."

"Very funny," Jack said. "Listen, I've got one idea I think we ought to consider. A Youth Auxiliary for kids that are under eighteen."

They all looked at him.

He said, "I've got a younger brother, seventeen years old. Freddy's an aggressive little bastard and dominates the local Boy Scouts. We could recruit him first of all. They'd all have to pay their five pseudo-dollars to join, but then only two a month since a kid only gets half as much GAI as an adult."

Jed said skeptically, "How else could we milk it?"

"Hell, we could have official uniforms, official knives, official tents. We'd milk it the same way that the Boy Scouts milk the little suckers."

"What'd we call it?" Karen said.

"The Subversive Scouts of America," Jack told her. "The Boy Scouts is a sissy organization. Helping old ladies across the street, Scout's honor, Scout's oath, all that sort of curd. That doesn't have any appeal to kids. All those sissy merit badges they have to work for, how to tie knots and so forth. Kids love violence. Look at the kind of Tri-Di shows and movies they prefer. We'll give 'em merit badges in karate, Kodakan Judo, Chinese Kempo, Jujitsus, Hoppa Ken, Nanpa Ken, rifle and pistol and possibly submachine gun marksmanship, boxing, wrestling, bullfighting..."

"Bullfighting!" Dick blurted.

Jack nodded at him. "Bullfighting. Why not? We'll get a bunch of overgrown calves and clip their horns down to the nubbin. Hell, that's the kind of animals they're fighting in Spain and Mexico these days, anyhow."

"Sounds good to me," Morris said. "If there's no objection, Jack'll start things rolling with this kid brother of his. What else?"

Karen said, "We're going to have to get the queer vote. The country's full of queers. We'd never come to power without getting their support."

"Make homosexuality legal between consenting adults, eh?" Jed said thoughtfully. "Like in England."

"Not just consenting adults and homos, all queers," Karen said. "Let them molest small children, practice sadism and maschonism, expose themselves in public, the works. Making it legal, for the first time since Ancient Greece, will probably clear it up in the long run. One of its biggest appeals is that it's illegal, something like Prohibition driving a lot of people to drink who ordinarily wouldn't have. It became all the thing."

She tried to drive home her point. "So far as molesting children is concerned, they're at the sexiest age of all. Always indulging in sex play as soon as they're old enough to finger themselves. Sadism? Let those who want to beat the hell out of each other, or maschonists be beaten, as long as they want. Maybe they'll finish each other off. It couldn't happen to nicer people."

Karen was now in full stride. "Let homos screw each other, or whatever their particular bit is, until hell freezes over. Who cares? At least they don't perpetuate themselves. Maybe that's a law we should pass *after* we get in. Queers, duly registered, will not be allowed to screw the opposite sex, and pass on their genes. Oscar Wilde had two kids for instance. I'm of the opinion that making it legal would be the eventual death blow to homosexuality. The thing is that a woman has better equipment for the sex act with a normal man. Take away the romance of being a queer because it's illegal and there's more fun in screwing a woman than a man."

"How about Lesbians?" Jed said.

"Even more so with Lesbians. Who can settle for a tongue job when there are six inches of penis— and up?"

"Up what?" Morris Malone said mildly.

"I meant longer. What anybody can do with a penis more than six inches long I've never been able to figure out, but some seem to have the dream that the longer the better."

Jack said, "As far as that molesting of children is concerned, it's been my experience that it's the other way around. Once a kid niece of mine climbed into my bed when I was supposedly taking a nap and . . ."

"Spare us," Karen said.

"Well, I didn't do anything, damn it. I just had to escape her. She knew what I had and she wanted to play around with it."

Morris Malone said, "All right, we'll make a play for the queer vote. Anything else?"

Karen said, "I had one more thing. Old age. There's too damn many old people in the country and most of them have a lousy time anyway. So what we advocate is that when anyone reaches sixty from then on he or she can opt for euthanasia, or whatever they call it. If they do, they're given a badge which informs one and all that they can do no wrong. Each man is given two beautiful girls— if he wants them; each woman, two gigolos. They don't have to pay anything in restaurants, hotels, shops, bars, or for transportation. They get the best food and guzzle available. At the end of a year of this, if they've survived, they're given a mickey and buried with honors."

Morris winced. "Wouldn't that lose us a lot of the elderly vote, before we come to power and can implement it?"

"Hell no. It'd be voluntary."

Jed said, "What'd we get out of it? The theory is we don't advocate anything unless there's a pseudo-dollar in it."

Karen was indignant. "We'd save all the Guaranteed Annual Income they'd ordinarily get. Hell, some of the old bastards live to be ninety or more."

Morris looked at her sadly. He said, "Listen, do you have any more far out ideas?"

"Just one more. As soon as we get in, send a firing squad to every insane asylum, hospital for incurables and old people's homes and mercifully execute them and about eighty-five percent of the guards, nurses and officials in charge."

This time, all four of the men winced in pain.

Dick Oppenheimer knew that if he was going to keep his in with this group he'd have to come up with some ideas too. He said, "I think I've got a suggestion."

"Let's hear it," Jack said. "I'm afraid to hear any more from our sweet leader of the Subversivettes."

Dick said, "Narcotics."

"What about them?" Jed said.

"Well, there's a lot of dopers in this country. We could use their votes. What we'd do is advocate that all narcotics be made legal. Let anybody who wants to blow his brains do it. Small loss anyway. They'd be available in any drugstore, at cost."

"Our angle?" Jed said.

"We'd put a one hundred percent tax on narcotics. They'd still be a fraction of the cost junkies pay the Mafia for them. But there's another angle, very idealistic on our part. Any addict who came to a hospital or institution to be treated, gets cured and then given a shot that makes him allergic to all narcotics for the rest of his life."

Jack scowled at him, and said, "Is there any such shot available?"

"Not that I know of," Dick told him, "but we could put the double-dome research doctors on it. They already have one for guzzle, Anabus. You take an Anabus pill and for at least three days you simply can't touch alcohol. If you so much as take a bite of fruitcake that's been soaked in brandy or rum you get sick as a dog."

"Holy Jumping Zoroaster," Jack said. "I'll have to remember the name of that drug— and stay away from it. I haven't obstained from guzzle for three days in a row since I was sixteen."

# 8

Dick Oppenheimer entered his apartment, closed the door behind him and then locked it. He went through the place, room by room, checking closets, under the bed, any other unlikely location where a person could have easily hidden. He found no one, of course.

He brought forth his electronic mop and went through the apartment again, sweeping it even more carefully than he had the conference room of the Subversive Party headquarters. He detected no bugs and returned to the living room. He went over to the desk and sat at it and brought forth the special transceiver that Walter Hardenberg, had issued him, flicked open its cover, activated it and propped it against the desk's phone screen.

He said carefully, "Clifford Dix, calling Director Hardenberg. Clifford Dix, Calling Walter Hardenberg."

After a time, the small screen of the transceiver lit up and the tight, fat, arrogant face of the IBI head was there. He said, "All right, Dix. Report."

Cliff Dix said, "Chief, this is more serious than I at first thought."

"How do you mean?"

"They're not serious."

The other looked at him, as though he was out of

his mind. He said, "What in the name of Holy Zoroaster are you talking about?"

"The heads of the Subversive Party. They aren't serious. They're just in this for something to do. They're bored. All three of them are on Guaranteed Annual Income and they haven't anything to do, so they came up with this little romp. Remember you told me to read up on former radical parties of the United States; the Wobblies, the commies, the various socialists and so forth? Well, all those people were idealists, devoted. They really believed in what they were advocating. They might have been wrong, or impractical, or whatever, but they believed in it. The same applied to revolutionary organizations in other countries. Len and Trotsky were dedicated idealists, if we like it or not. In the French Revolution so were Robespierre, Danton and Marat. In the American Revolution, so were Tom Paine, Jefferson, Madison and the rest. The nearest thing to an opportunist was possibly Aaron Burr."

The other was scowling at him. "Get to the point. And these people?"

"I don't know about the rank and file membership but the three leaders are making this up as they go along. Their whole program. They're taking it off the tops of their heads. By the way, they aren't a bunch of crackpots in the ordinary sense of the word. They're all smart and with better than average educations and intellectual backgrounds."

Hardenberg was still scowling, as though he couldn't believe any of what his agent was telling him. He said, "How do you mean they're making it up as they go along? What's their program?"

"It's still half-formed and most of it's fantastic, but they're appealing to just about every element in the country from hopheads to homosexuals. In the past, minority parties appealed to one segment of the population or the other, to the working class, to Blacks, to anti-Semites, or whatever. This group is trying to appeal to everybody. They've even started a woman's auxiliary and a youth auxillary."

His chief thought about it. "Why do you consider it more serious than you first thought? It sounds to me as though they're half-baked."

"Sir," Cliff Dix said, "the thing is that it isn't just them. The whole country's bored. People as a whole don't have anything to do. GAI supplies them with just enough to get by and to keep them in trank or beer as they watch Tri-Di. Anything that comes along that offers excitement, something different, has appeal. The members are beginning to roll in and it'll mushroom as soon as this policy of not allowing anyone to become a Full Member until he's recruited two more Candidate Members takes hold."

"Is that why you wanted me to have two more agents signed up here in Greater Washington?"

"Yes."

Hardenberg sighed. "Who's the head of it?"

"There is no head. There's a triumvirate that seems to make ultimate decisions but one doesn't seem to wield any more power than either of the others."

"Doesn't there seem to be any conflict of interest? Something we could work on, drive a wedge between them?"

"Not that I've noted thus far. From what I gather, all four on the National Executive Committee are old acquaintances and close friends. Besides, none of them seem to be particularly ambitious."

"Not ambitious!" his chief blurted in indignation.

"Are you drivel-happy, Dix? They're trying to take over the country."

"Yes, but as I keep saying, largely from sheer boredom, not ambition. There's another angle that ought to be mentioned. In the past, radical parties were usually composed of working people who had to hold down their jobs and hence didn't have much time to devote to party work. But most of the converts to the Subversive Party seem to be on GAI and hence have all the time in the world. Practically all Party members will be able to devote full time to recruiting and so forth."

"What's this National Executive Committee you mentioned?"

"It's evidently the ruling committee of the organization, though there doesn't seem to be any Party constitution. It's composed of the three members of the Triumvirate, Karen Landy, head of the Subversivettes, the women's auxiliary, and myself, the National Organizer."

"*Yourself!*"

"Yes, sir. You told me to get as high in Party ranks as possible. I'm as high as possible. As National Organizer I have to go about the country forming branches."

His boss scowled again. "Wouldn't you be in a better position to check on them there at headquarters in Center City?"

"Possibly, but it was the only manner in which I could become a member of the NEC. Besides, it'll give me a chance to check up on how it's progressing nationally, get an idea of the membership in other areas, that sort of thing. What I suggest you do, sir, is send the two agents I supposedly recruited here to join the local branch, when it's formed. To be effective, and possibly rise in the ranks, they have to become Full Members and possibly later, Senior Members. That means each will have to recruit first two Candidate Members and later five more."

"And they in turn will have to do the same?"

"That's right, sir. If they're to become Full Members."

"At that rate, we'll have every damned agent in the IBI in the Subversive Party!"

"Yes, sir. If they're to be effective, they have to become at least Full Members."

"I'll think about it. Anything else, Dix?"

"Yes, sir. I suggest that the two agents you send here to Center City to take my place be heavies."

"Heavies? How do you mean?"

"I mean tough boys, from the Department of Dirty Tricks. So far, there's been no indication that the Triumvirate will advocate force and violence, but they're already recruiting a sort of storm trooper group called the Minute Men, or Suede Shirts, and have decided to form a youth group to be called the Subversive Scouts. We might need some muscle, before we're through."

"Very well, Dix," the older man said. "I must compliment you on your performance thus far. To be a member of the ruling committee already is no small accomplishment. Keep in constant touch with me on new developments."

"Yes, sir."

The other's face faded.

Dick Oppenheimer stared at the transceiver screen for a long moment, then sighed and took the instrument up, deactivated it and returned it to his pocket.

He flicked on the phone screen, dialed the

National Data Banks and said, "I want the Dossier Complete of Karen Landy. I don't know her Identification Number but she is evidently a resident of Center City."

"Do you have the priority to request a citizen's Dossier Complete?"

He went through the routine of putting his IBI card in the screen's slot and, shortly, there before him began flashing the life of Karen Landy.

After that, he got the Dossier Complete of Frederic Zieglar, brother of Jack Zieglar, Boy Scout and future leader of the Subversive Scouts. He had a little bit more luck with Freddy. On his Crime Dossier he had two bits of business. He had once evidently participated in stealing a hovercar to go on a pleasure ride with some of his friends. And also had participated in a gang-bang of a fourteen year old girl. It turned out later that the girl had been banged before, gang and otherwise, but it was on Freddy's record.

Karen was another thing. She was as clean as driven snow, as the expression went, so far as her dossier revealed.

He leaned back and thought about it. Of what he had seen of Karen Landy, she didn't seem exactly that clean, even by modern codes of morality.

# 9

Professor Bruce Winecoup of the Subversive Party think tank said into the microphone before him, "So now I bring you Comate Jeremiah Kleiser of the National Executive Committee." He turned and smiled at Jed and relinquished his place and resumed his own chair.

Jed got up, took his place on the podium and looked out over the auditorium. There were approximately a thousand students, professors and instructors in the audience. Ordinarily, he knew, the students largely did their studies in the privacy of their own quarters, but the University City was maintained for its libraries, its laboratories, its physical education and sports facilities, for the few live lectures like this one, and for a rallying point where students could exchange ideas— and throw beer busts— in the old tradition of colleges.

He nodded and said, "First of all, I wish to point out that our organization is not without notable precedent in its position.

"It was George Washington who said, 'The basis of our political system is the right of the people to make and to alter their constitutions of government.'

"And it was James Madison, fifth President of the United States and Father of the American Constitution, who said, 'We are free today substantially; but the day will come when our Republic will be an impossibility. It will be an impossibility because wealth will become concentrated in the hands of a few. A Republic cannot exist upon bayonets; and when that day comes, then we must rely upon the wisdom of the best elements in the country to readjust the laws of the nation to the changed conditions.'

"Nor should we forget Abraham Lincoln in his First Inaugural Address: 'This country, with its institutions, belongs to the people who inhabit it. Whenever they shall grow weary of the existing government, they can exercise the constitutional right of amending it, or their revolutionary right to dismember or overthrow it.'"

Jed looked out over his audience for a long moment before going on. "I think the point is made. We have the *right* to make any changes the majority wishes. What we need now is the might to back it up."

A student in the front row called up, "Sure. But suppose your Subversive Party was elected and you tried to put over all these changes you advocate. The Supreme Court would declare them all unconstitutional and that'd be that."

Jed laughed and said, "The hell with the Supreme Court. The moment we get in, we're going to declare the Constitution unconstitutional and abolish it and with it all of its institutions, including the Supreme Court. Why should a handful of old men, none of them elected to office by the people, be able to dictate to the country? The Constitution was written for a bunch of farmers over two hundred years ago, and no matter how much patching up with amendments, scotch tape and baling wire has taken place over the centuries, it's still nonsense in this day and age. Was it Madison or Jefferson who thought it should be completely rewritten every twenty years?"

He went on with the talk, presenting the Subversive Party program in such manner as he thought would appeal to students and their teachers.

At the end, he said, "There are four Party members at desks in the rear of the hall. Anyone wishing to join up as a Candidate Member today can fill out a membership blank immediately after the meeting, pay his initiation fee and make any other donations he sees fit. This is it, ladies and gentlemen, the new party on its way to the top. I suggest that you get in on the ground floor. Thank you."

There was considerable applause, a few boos.

Professor Bruce Winecoup came to his feet, rubbing his hands happily. He had been assured by Jed that if more than five students signed up they would be considered the professor's converts and he would be promoted to Senior Member and, since the think tank was already overflowing, Winecoup would be named chairman of a second think tank.

Even from the rostrum, Jed could see lines forming before the four desks.

Morris Malone was being interviewed by a Tri-Di commentator with a national following and playing it very sincere.

The commentator said, "Then what it amounts to is that you plan to declare adulterants illegal, Mr. Malone."

"That is exactly right, Mr. Black. Take but one example: the candy, ice cream and other sweets we feed our children. In the old days, candy bars were made from pure sugar and honey, good chocolate, fresh nuts and fruits and so forth. Ice cream was made of real milk and cream, real sugar, real vanilla beans, fresh strawberries, and other flavorings. Today, saccharin, synthetic vanilla, adulterated chocolate, soy bean milk, and less than nourishing fillers have taken over. We advocate returning to quality in every commodity produced. We will simply not produce inferior products. Everything will be the best possibly to manufacture or grow. This is a waste system today, the only motivation is profit. We will eat the best food possible to produce, wear the best clothes and shoes, live in the best houses possible to build. Why, take just that last example. In George Washington's time they were able to build good houses many of which still stand today. But look at the houses going up now. The buyer is lucky if they stand long enough for the mortgage to be paid off. A housing development is often a slum before it's completed. Yet approximately the same amount of material goes into a house today as did at the time of the American Revolution, over two hundred years ago."

The commentator nodded. "And this campaign of yours against waste, how does it apply to such union activities as featherbedding?"

"Featherbedding will be illegal and punishable," Morris told him. "All make-work will be eliminated. All planned obsolescence as well. Any inventor, factory manager, or anyone else who comes up with some planned obsolescence bit is to be thrown in the slammer."

"I see," Ted Black said. "And, tell me, Mr. Malone, how is your new organization progressing? It would seem to me that you are treading rather ruthlessly on a good many toes, attacking a good many of our cherished traditions."

Morris shook his head very earnestly indeed. "Not at all. There are some malcontents, of course, who oppose us. For instance, using the same example I just went over, candy manufacturers who make huge profits by turning out adulterated products that rot out the teeth of our young ones. However, largely our program is being received with open arms. You see, when a social change is pending it is not simply one element in the population that trends toward it, but most, if not all, elements. Farmers would like to return to producing the wonderful fruits and vegetables our grandfathers knew and cut down on insecticides and artificial fertilizers. Construction workers would rather construct houses they could be proud of. Autohover workers would prefer to build adequate vehicles rather than the monstrosities manufactured today. Doctors and nurses would prefer to get off the assembly line that medicine has become today and return to an era when there was more personal contact between doctor and patient.

"You must realize that farmers too must eat the inadequate food they are growing. Construction workers live in the same type of houses they build. Autohover workers drive the cars they make. Doctors and other health workers wind up in the hands of practitioners like themselves when they become ill. And manufacturers breathe the same air they pollute and cannot fish or swim in our rivers, lakes or oceans when on vacation. All suffer under this insane system of waste and pollution. I could go on and on."

The commentator sent his eyes up to the studio clock and said, "Unfortunately, Mr. Malone, our time is just about up." He looked into one of the Tri-Di camera lenses. "Folks, if you are interested in getting more information on the Subversive Party and its stand, you can write simply to The Subversive Party, Center City; no more address is required."

The red light above the clock went out, indicating that the studio was no longer hot.

Ted Black, the commentator, rubbed the back of his neck wearily and turned to Morris Malone. He said, his voice wry, "You haven't got a membership blank on you, have you?"

Karen Landy had wound up her lecture and was now taking questions. She fielded them herself, rather than taking them through the chairwoman.

Before her were some five hundred women of all ages, though the twenty to thirty year span predominated. About a hundred of these wore the striking new suede uniform dresses of the Subversivettes. Karen knew the setup. Female Party members had brought friends and acquaintances to the meeting in hopes of signing them up as Candidate Members and thus winning credit toward achieving Full Membership or even, in some cases, Senior Membership. A good many of the new converts were on the ambitious side, particularly those who had formerly been active in the women's lib groups.

There was an upraised hand, which she acknowledged, and a voice from halfway back through the audience called, "You mentioned the fact that for several thousand years men have dominated women. Was it ever any different?"

Karen said definitely, "it most certainly was. Any competent student of anthropology will tell you that for the overwhelmingly greater history of the human race we lived under matriarchy. Read such books as *The Motherright*, Frazer's *The Golden Bough*, Robert Graves' works, especially, *The Greek Myths*, above all, Morgan's *Ancient Society*. The human race has existed for tens of thousands of years, more or less in its present form. Only in the last few thousand did patriarchal society take over from women who formerly dominated clan and tribe."

"Why?" somebody called out. "Why did it change?"

Karen said, "Because of the development of the tool and also the larger domesticated animals. Women, as a rule, were not able to use the new heavy metal tools due to the long months of pregnancy and then the need to take care of the new infant. Men took over agriculture and the flocks and became the providers. He who controls a person's means of subsistence controls that person. And with the coming of private property in the lands, in the flocks, in the mines, a new question arose. A man wanted to be assured that his property was inherited by his own children, especially his sons. So new laws, new customs, new codes of morality were evolved to assure this. Marriage, for one, and the demand that a woman be a virgin upon marriage and then that she remain faithful to her spouse all her life. It went to the extreme in some lands of harems being established and seraglios which the wives were not allowed to leave. Our position in society reached its nadir."

"So why are things going to be different now?" another voice called.

"Because we are no longer unable to handle the tool. The tool of today is automated. Usually, you need only press a button, activate a switch, check out some meters and gauges, program a computer. Any woman can do this at least as well as a man. We are not dependent upon them for our subsistance. Even if unemployed we are as eligible for GAI as are the men. For the first time since ancient times we are free. We even have the vote now, and, fellow women..." Karen paused dramatically "...we outnumber them."

A cheer arose.

Another hand went up and Karen acknowledged it.

The questioner asked, "What is the Subversive Party's stand on religion?"

"A strong one," Karen said, making her voice strong. "Modern-day religions are antiquated and many have become outright rackets. The largest are patriarchies, not even allowing women to hold higher ranks such as priests, rabbis, or, in the Mohammedan religion an Imam. When the White Goddess, who dominated religion throughout the Mediterranean region and beyond in ancient times, was overthrown by the patriarchal Aryans, such as the Greeks, a new pantheon of gods took over. Zeus replaced Hera, who was a manifestation of the White Goddess, and since then women assumed a minor role in religion. The White Goddess was far, far more spiritual than the lusty, lecherous, drunken Greek gods who took her place. The early mysteries were based on her tenets and never has man reached a higher ethic.

"The matter will have to be explored further, perhaps. Who can say but that we might return to the faith of the White Goddess, those among us who wish to retain a faith? There are more women, as I have said, than men. And what woman, now liberated, wants to worship an old geezer with white beard? Hera, Diana and Pallas Athene, all representing the White Goddess in one of her three manifestations were beautiful goddesses. Why not consider their ancient teachings and mysteries again?"

A laugh went through the audience and some clapped.

Karen wound it up. "It is even suggested that we have written a new set of Ten Commandments. Most of them, at least, are antiquated, dealing either with worship of the man god, or with matters of private property— including wives and maid servants, which are lumped together with a man's donkey as his property."

Jack Zieglar, brave in his Minute Man outfit, came zooming up to the parking area of the Center City Hoverbike and Racing Club, on his spanking new light suede colored hoverbike.

He had purposedly arrived about ten minutes late so that tardy club members wouldn't be coming in and interrupting proceedings while he was holding forth.

Two club members, who had obviously been appointed a committee, came up to him and shook hands. He looked out over the gathering. There must have been at least two hundred of them. At least three quarters were young men, although there was a smattering of girls. He hadn't thought about that. Would there be a woman's auxiliary of the Minute Men Hoverbike Corps? Or should he turn that over to Karen Landy? It would have to be brought up in the next convening of the National Executive Committee.

His two greeters conducted him to an improvised stand. One of them mounted it and held up his hands for silence.

When it was finally achieved, he called, "I'll make this short. You've all heard of the new Subversive

Party and its Minute Men. This evening we have with us National Executive Committee member Jack Zieglar, Commander in Chief of the Minute Men. Comate Zieglar!"

Jack Zieglar looked at the chairman from the side of his eyes. Comate yet. Evidently, this one was already a party member. He wondered who had signed him up.

He spoke into the improvised public address system mike. "I'm going to start this off with the nitty-gritty. One of our slogans is, *What's In It For Me?* In short, what does Number One— you— get out of joining the Minute Men and the Subversive Party? The answer is, plenty.

"In the whole history of political parties, new and old, there's never been one that lays it on the line like we do. We're not out promising pie in the sky. We're not out to uplift the poor, or better the lot of the downtrodden, working class or otherwise. We're not out to end wars, or erase racial differences. We're not a party for youth, or the aged, or anybody else who thinks they're under-privileged.

"We're all in this for Number One."

He paused as a murmur went through them—a somewhat surprised murmur.

"Of course," he went on, "the program of the Subversive Party *will* aid all of these groups and more. But that is secondary to the point. The point is that we're out for *us*. We're going to clean up this country in more ways than one. And when we're through we'll all be breathing decent air, swimming in our lakes and rivers and fishing in them. We'll be eating decent food, drinking decent guzzle. And we won't be getting robbed by the Establishment. Hell, *we'll* be the Establishment, especially those who get in on the ground floor, who join up in these early days.

"Now, let me say a few words about this Minute Man organization. We'll all go around on the official suede colored hoverbikes, all dressed in this uniform you see me in. We're going to be tough, but we're going to avoid violence. We don't want any rumbles with the john-fuzz. What we're going to be is polite but efficient. We're going to lead the parades, police the meetings and rallies, usher at the hall meetings and conventions. We're going to be the pride of the Subversive Party.

"Now, each one who joins up joins as a sergeant and is entitled to wear three stripes, that's our lowest rank. Later on, as some of you become Senior Members, you'll be promoted to lieutenant and later captain or major and so on up. Promotions in this outfit are going to come fast. And, of course, the officers will be put on the payroll. The pay, even at the beginning, will be higher than you get on Guaranteed Annual Income." He grinned at them. "I told you our slogan is *What's In It For Me?*

"As soon as you've gotten some background in the organization, some of the Senior Members will be promoted still further and sent to other cities to organize local troops of the Minute Men. The faster and the bigger we get the more there'll be in it for each of us. Needless to say, when we finally come to power, and at the rate the Party is booming that won't be long, we'll be in the catbird seat."

He looked at them very confidentially and said slowly, "In connection with that slogan of ours, *What's In It For Me,* and you joining up while the organization is in its infancy, let me give you another slogan. *The Dog that Snaps the Quickest Gets the Bone*."

The meeting, in all, took almost three hours and the day was waning by the time Jack Zieglar had answered the last questions. He was exhausted, particularly since he had come in the first place with the remnants of a headache left over from the night before.

He got a sheaf of membership blanks from a saddlebag of his hoverbike and handed them over to the chairman of the meeting. "You can distribute these, Comate," he said. "I assume tou know the procedure of joining up new Candidate Members."

"Yes, Comate," the other said crisply. "An I hope to make Senior Member tonight."

"Wizard," Jack said, just as crisply. "Carry on, Minute Man."

And he was off in a zoom.

# 10

Jack Zieglar zoomed exactly as far as the nearest automated bar, four or five streets down. He parked his vehicle in the back and entered and went to the rear and took an empty table. There were only a few other customers this early in the evening.

He looked at the sterile establishment. Calling it a bar was a leftover from the old days. There was no bar in the ordinary sense of the word. There were just tables.

He decided that it was something to take up with Mo and Jed. Work into their program the need to end some of this damned automation. Bars should have bartenders, restaurants should have waiters. There should be that personal touch. You can go too far in saving labor.

He dialed a pseudo-whiskey, after putting his Universal Credit Card in the table's payment slot and sighed when the table top sank down to return with the drink. He should have ordered a double while he was at it. He rectified that the next time around.

A stranger slipped into the chair across from him. A neat, conservatively dressed stranger, rather bland of face, chunky of figure and running about forty years of age. Jack couldn't put his finger on it, but for some reason he didn't like the other's looks.

He said, ungraciously, "There are other tables, most of them empty.

The newcomer nodded agreement and said, "I wanted to talk to you. You're John Zieglar."

"That's right. What did you want to talk about?"

"The Subversive Party."

"Oh," Jack said. "Sorry I was abrupt. I'm a little tired. Just came from a meeting."

"Yes, I know. I was there. In the background. Interesting talk, Mr. Zieglar."

"Thanks," Jack said. "Were you considering joining? Have a drink."

"No thank you. And in answer to your first question, not exactly."

"Then what did you want to talk about?"

"Five thousand pseudo-dollars."

"Well, that makes interesting conversation," Jack admitted, dialing still another whiskey. "What about five thousand pseudo-dollars? You know, I don't believe I've ever had five thousand pseudo-dollars in one chunk in my life."

"That's what I assumed. I want to deposit it to your credit account in the National Data Banks."

Jack looked at him for a long moment before saying, "Why?"

"In return for a service."

"All right, what service?"

The other leaned back. "You're a member of the National Executive Committee of the Subversive Party. I represent someone who would like to be in on the secret decisions made by that committee."

"What secret decisions?"

The other looked at him as though Jack wasn't quite with it and said, "Any secret decisions. The latest plans. The latest tactics the organization decides to pursue. We want someone on the very inside."

"Whom do you represent?"

The other's face reflected marytrdom. "Now please, Mr. Zieglar."

"How in the hell could I report any secret decisions to you if I don't even know who you are, or where you are?"

"You don't contact us. We periodically contact you."

Jack thought about it and, while he thought, finished his drink. He was beginning to feel them.

The other urged, "You said your slogan was *What's In It For Me?* Well, for starters, five thousand pseudo-dollars. Possibly there'll be more later, if you come through satisfactorily."

"All right, it's a deal."

The stranger brought out his own credit card and stuck it in the slot of the table's phone screen. "If you will," he said.

Jack took his card from the payment slot and put it into the phone screen along with the other's.

The stranger said, "Please transfer five thousand pseudo-dollars from this account to that of John Zieglar."

"Carried out," the computer voice said.

The other came to his feet. "I'll be getting in touch with you. I'll use the code name Bing."

"Okay, Bing," Jack said. He watched the other turn and leave the automated bar.

He shrugged and dialed another drink in the way of celebration.

He hadn't finished this one before another stranger loomed over him. In fact, three of them, the other two flanking the first and slightly behind him.

They were all burly specimens and not particularly reassuring of face. All three affected costumes similar to those worn by most of the members of the Center City Hoverbike and Racing Club, featuring a black leather jacket and a crash helmet.

The first one said nastily, "On your feet, *Comate* Zieglar. We wanta talk to you."

Jack tried to keep slur from his voice. "About what?" he said. "I'm busy."

The other looked down at the drink and sneered, "You look busy. Come on, you cloddy. Up on your feet, or we'll slap you up."

"If you want to talk to me, why not sit down and talk? Maybe I'll even listen," Jack said, in attempted bravado. There were three of them and all of them cold sober and all of them at least his size. And all of them obviously pissed off about something or other.

"Because we want to talk to you outside," one of the flanking two growled. "More privacy, see?"

The leader of the three added to that, "Quit stalling, *Comate*."

The bar was completely automated. There were no waiters or bartenders or anyone else who worked there in sight. Any personnel was behind the scenes. The only others present were drinkers, and most of them at distant tables, since Jack had deliberately chosen one in the back. A couple were staring over at the discussion going on, but they most certainly didn't look the types that would respond to a call for aid.

Jack came to his feet. "Wizard," he said. "Let's go and have this talk. It'd better be good."

"Oh, it'll be very good, *Comate*," the leader said.

He led the way toward the door, Jack followed,

nervous at the fact that the other two goons were behind him where he couldn't see.

The parking lot was behind the automated bar. They headed for it and to a shadowed spot.

The leader turned and faced Jack Zieglar and at the same moment a shattering blow landed on the back of Jack's neck. He went sprawling to the ground.

The leader snapped, "Get up. There's more coming."

Jack said, rubbing his neck, "I'm happy where I am for the time being. What in the name of the Holy Zoroaster is going on?"

"We might as well tell you now, while you can still understand," the other said. "I'm president of the Hoverbike Club. These two boys are the treasurer and the secretary. It's a good club and we like our jobs. Consequently, we don't like you, *Comate*—Commander in Chief of the Minute Men. And we don't need you sucking around trying to steal our membership away from us."

"Besides that," one of the others said, "we don't like what you had to say about this here country and the gov'ment. We don't like nobody says anything against the gov'ment."

"That's too bad," Jack said. "But we've still got freedom of speech in the United States."

One of them kicked him in the right thigh, none too gently.

"All right, that does it," Jack muttered, coming slowly erect. "Here goes nothing." Both his neck and especially his leg ached excruciatingly but he made it to his feet.

The three stood back for a moment, letting him

get straight up and all three laughing lowly and in anticipation.

"I'll take first crack," the leader said, moving in confidently, balled fists advanced efficiently. Oh, he'd used his hands before.

Jack in his military training had had some, not a great deal, of hand to hand combat. He had no intention of following the rules once, long ago, set down by the Marquis of Queensberry. He cursed his fate that his right leg was so numb that he wouldn't be able to use his karate kicks. Relying largely on his left leg for balance, he bunched up his right hand, spear-like, with fingers straight forward, rather than in a fist, and launched forward for the other's solar plexus, just at the moment that a heavy blow struck him on his left shoulder.

But the other staggered back, his hands now over his belly, his face ashen.

"Get him!" he gasped.

And the other two came boring forward.

Jack took two or three blows, returned blows as best he could and then went down again.

The two hoverclub officers advanced, obviously with the intention of giving him the boot— he noted dully that they were very heavy boots. He tried to roll away, but was already too beaten up to have any dexterity remaining.

"Let him have it boys," the club president gasped. "The funker don't fight fair."

Jack took exactly one kick to his side before the situation altered. Of a sudden, there were others on the scene. How many others he didn't know, but there seemed to be enough of them.

And it was then that the fog rolled in, compounded of the blows he had taken and the guzzle consumed in the bar.

When it rolled out again, his head was in some stranger's lap and half a dozen others were standing around.

He managed to get out, "What in the hell happened?"

"We ran the bastards off, Comate, after, uh, chastising them a little," his rescuer said.

And then Jack dimly remembered him. It was one of the two committee men who had presided at the meeting at the Center City Hoverbike Club.

The other was going on. "We thought they were up to something, particularly when over half the boys joined up. They got together and were whispering around, so we followed them. They waited outside the bar here and so did we— across the street where they couldn't see us. They were evidently waiting for you to come out. When you didn't, they went in to get you. When they started working you over, we headed in. You put up a pretty good show while it lasted, Comate."

"Thanks," Jack said. He staggered to his feet and went over to vomit against the wall of the building. The others looked on sympathetically.

The Party member said worriedly, "Can we see you home, Comate? I'm afraid you may have taken a broken rib from that kick."

"All right," Jack managed to say. "But I don't think I'll be able to tool my bike."

"Leave it here. You can ride behind me. I hope you can stand the jogging. I'll take it easy."

He did try to take it easy, but a couple of times along the way Jack was afraid he might faint and fall off.

When they got to his small suburban house two of

them helped him inside. The others stayed outside, evidently as guards.

The Party member said. "They'll stay outside for the rest of the night, Comate. Just in case those funkers round up some reinforcements and try to take another crack at you."

They got him to the couch in the living room and one went into the bath and returned with some iodine, a wet cloth and a towel. Jack submitted to the first aid treatment. He hadn't realized that he had taken cuts and bruises on his face and hands when he had fallen to the gravel of the parking lot.

He said, "You boys help yourselves to a drink over at the autobar. Here's my credit card."

"You want one, Comate?" one of the two said, heading for the bar.

Jack recognized him now. It was the other committee member.

He said, "No, I've had one. It's all been puked up by now, but I don't feel like any more."

When the other two were seated across from him, drinks in hand, he looked at them. Nice looking kids in their mid-twenties.

He said, "Those new Candidate Members you took in tonight. They'll count on your record. You're now Senior Members."

"Well, they weren't really our recruits, Comate Zieglar. Really they were yours."

"They'll count as yours. Are you both on GAI?"

"Yes, sir," they answered in unison.

"Well, from now on you're on the Subversive Party payroll as captains of the Minute Men. Your pay will be two hundred pseudo-dollars a week. That'll be upped, of course, as soon as the treasury fattens."

They gawked at him.

"I told you that we're in this for ourselves," Jack told them. "Report in the morning to the National Office for your assignments. We need dedicated Minute Men. At first you'll probably be put to work organizing the local troop. Then, most likely, you'll be sent into the field to organize other troops. Then, of course, you'll be on expense account."

# 11

Jack Zieglar took the following two days off to recover from his beating.

On the third day, when he entered the National Office in the late morning, he was taken aback to find a number of others behind desks in his supposed office. And, for that matter, out in the halls. The place was bustling. Most were strangers to Jack, and most of the men wore suede shirts and most of the girls suede dresses.

He went into Jed's office and found no Jed, but another three desks moved into that room, not to mention a few business machines muttering away. He hadn't the vaguest idea of their nature, nor what they were muttering about.

He went to the conference room and there was Jed, looking harassed with a pile of papers.

Jed looked up and said, "Where in the hell have you been and what in the hell's happened to you?"

Jack said, "I ran into some people who don't like the Subversive Party. Happily, I was rescued by some who do."

Jed said, "Tell me about it later. Meanwhile, I have some of the damnedest news. Some rich old coot out on the West Coast, a crackpot on ecology, has just donated fifty thousand pseudo-dollars."

Jack whistled. "Fifty thousand!"

"That's right. Other donations are coming in, but that's the big one."

Jack said, "That's good. I just hired two Senior Members at two hundred a week."

Jed stared at him. "You *did?* Why?"

"Because they're bully boys. We're going to need bully boys. Don't you see what my face looks like?"

Morris Malone came in with a sheaf of papers in hand looking as though he had been up all night. He said, "I wonder if we ought to bring Dick Oppenheimer back here. These new towns coming in with more than five members apiece are so many he can't possibly go about organizing them all."

"So what do we do, Mo?" Jed said.

"Like we said earlier. We bring him back to be First National Organizer and start putting together a team of National Organizers. He has the know-how now. Right as of this minute, we could use ten National Organizers. Before the week is out, probably twenty."

"Zoroaster!" Jack said.

Jed told Morris about the $50,000 donation.

Morris Malone thought about it. He said, "It's about time that we voted ourselves a salary. By the way, here's the first copy of the *Subversive Manifesto*. Sale price, ten pseudo-dollars. Maybe we ought to make it twenty. Every member *has* to read it, not counting anybody else who wants to. And we handle all sales."

"What kind of a salary?" Jed said.

Morris pursed his lips. "Say, a thousand pseudo-dollars a week for all Triumvirate members."

Jack pursed his lips in turn. "The treasury wouldn't last very long."

"The treasury is just beginning to pour in," Morris

Malone told him. "Can you imagine how our uniform rake-offs, our emblem cut, our new memberships, our donations, are accumulating. And now comes our first book."

Jack said, "I've got another one. The other night, just before I was worked over by three anti-Minute Men goons, I was given five thousand pseudo-dollars by some character who wanted me to report inside information on the Party."

Jed was fascinated. "What did you tell him? You know, I didn't believe it when Mo said we'd be offered bribes by government agents, the police and so forth."

"What'd'ya mean, what'd I tell him?" Jack said indignantly. "I took it, of course."

"Who was he?" Morris said.

"Beats me, Mo," Jack said. "He said that his code name would be Bing and he'd keep in touch."

"Well, what are you going to tell him?"

"What can I tell him? Anything he wants to know. We don't have any secrets."

Morris Malone thought about that for a moment. He said, finally, "You know, I was obliquely approached by some cloddy who hinted at the same thing. He never mentioned a definite sum but he was hinting. He had some sort of foreign accent."

Jed was intrigued. "What kind of a foreign accent?"

"I don't know. It wasn't French or Italian. I think I would have recognized those."

The three of them thought about it some more.

Jack said, "You know, I think I settled too cheaply. I should have held out."

Morris said, "Yeah. From now on, no member of the Triumvirate can sell out for less than fifty thousand pseudo-dollars. We can scale that down for members of the National Executive Committee. Maybe twenty-five thousand. Jack, what'd you do with the five thousand?"

"It's deposited to my account," Jack said.

Jed said, "Well, the hell with that. It's got to go into the kitty. Into the Subversive Party account."

"Screw you. I took that bribe on my own."

Morris said reasonably, "We can't handle it that way. We're all in this together. Switch it to the common account. When other bribes come in, we'll do the same. But I still say none of us sells out in the future for less than fifty thousand. Hell, we're not pikers."

"Okay," Jack said in resignation. "But I never had five thousand before in my life."

"You're an easy lay," Jed said. He cast his eyes upward in thought. "You know, we're going to get a lot of this. Not just American government agencies but foreign ones too, especially as the organization continues to grow. Take Canada to the north, Mexico to the south. Both of their economies are so tied in with that of America that they've just *got* to know what's going on here and what's going to happen."

Jack said, "Yeah, and the Soviet Complex. When they hear that there's a new radical outfit in America they're going to be jittering over whether or not we'll continue the detente if and when we get in. They'll want inside information, right from the horse's mouth, and we three are the horse's mouth."

"And Japan," Jed added happily. "America's their biggest customer. And Common Europe, they'll be jittering too."

"Well, we won't play any favorites," Jack said. "We'll let 'em all bribe us. Last night was the first time in my life I was ever bribed. I loved it."

Morris had long since thrown his sheaf of papers to the table and taken a chair. He said, "We're going to have to take over more office space. My office is so full of desks that I can hardly get into it. Karen is recruiting unemployed secretaries and stenographers like crazy. They're all on GAI and work for free, and are glad to have something to do. Isn't that suite across the hall empty?"

"I'll see about it," Jed said. "By the way, I hit on a new gimmick for raising funds. We'll have official funerals."

The other two looked at him.

He said, "Why let these morticians get the gravy for planting our faithful members? From now on, when a member in good standing kicks off he'll be given an honorary funeral by the Subversive Party. There'll be an honor guard of Minute Men. Some Senior Member will give a funeral oration. He'll be buried in a casket covered in suede. The grave stone will have the party emblem on it. We'll sell the survivors both the casket and the tombstone, at an inflated price. We'll have to make a deal with some casket manufacturer to produce our official caskets at a cut rate and the same with the tombstone cutters. After the funeral, there'll be a party and the Senior Member will give an inspiring talk about the deceased, and then take up a collection— for the Party fund."

Jack said, "Holy Zoroaster, have we no mercy anywhere along the line?"

Jed said, "No. If we're going to put this thing over, we've got to milk every angle. Even if we never do come to power, we've still got a good thing. A thousand pseudo-dollars a week. Wow!"

Mo said, "Talking about coming to power, we've got to start thinking in terms of contesting the next national election."

Jed ogled him, "Have you gone drivel-happy, Mo? How could we contest an election? Even with all the money pouring in, we don't begin to have the resources to contest a major election."

"It won't cost anything," Morris told him. "The government supplies the funds these days for campaigns. They have ever since those campaign donation scandles back in the late 1960s and early '70s. Any political party that puts up candidates in all the states in a national election has the campaign financed by the government— supposedly to prevent corruption. It hasn't made much difference in the past few elections since the Republican Party and the Democrat Party merged into the Democratic Republicans. For the first time in a long time they're going to have an election really contested— it won't just be a matter of Democratic Republican nominees fighting it out in the primaries. And we'll demand that the government finance our candidates the same as they do the Democratic Republicans."

While he was talking, Karen Landy had entered, also with a sheaf of papers in her hand, and had taken a seat. She looked over-worked.

Jed said thoughtfully, "One thing that'll save a lot of money campaigning is that we can demand free time on the Tri-Di radio networks. The law is that if you give time to one candidate, the opposing candidate can demand equal time."

"Who'll we have for candidates?" Jack said gloomily. "I sure as hell don't want to run for any office. None of us are competent enough to run the country."

"That's where you're wrong," Morris told him. "Politicians are seldom very competent men. Somerset Maugham once wrote, I think it was in *The Summing Up*, that in his time he'd met a good many politicians and to his surprise had found that they largely weren't very intelligent. He finally came to the conclusion that it didn't take intelligent men to run governments. As a matter of fact, to use one period of history as an example, neither Churchill, Roosevelt nor Stalin and certainly not Hitler, got high grades in school. Hitler couldn't even pass his art school entry examinations. President Grant graduated from West Point about half way down his class and later proved his lack of much intelligence in the White House when everybody in his Administration was on the take, except him. If he'd had any brains he would have been on the take too."

Jed said, "Yeah, but there's another angle to contesting the election and actually coming to power. Look what happens to those who get power. Look at the Kennedys. Look at the story of the Macedonians. Philip, the first one to come to power, was assassinated. Parmenion, his top general and largely responsible for the success of the Macedonian army, was killed by Alexander. Alexander died a 'natural' death by drinking himself into an early grave. So his son and wife were killed and then his team, Ptolemy, Antipater, Seleucus and the other generals, fought it out for decades to see who would take over his empire. And, after they had all been killed off, their sons took up the feud. Or look at the Roman Caesars. How many of them died in bed?"

Jack said, "He's got a point. And what's the use of our coming to power if we wind up getting clobbered? I was damn near clobbered a few nights ago, and we're not even in power yet."

Morris said, "Possibly our best bet is not to come to power, seemingly. We'll use some figureheads. If anybody gets nailed, it'll be them."

Karen Landy said, "Seems to me it's about time we decided what this new government of ours is going to look like." She turned to Morris Malone. "You're our theoretician, Mo. What happens after we declare the Constitution unconstitutional?"

Morris twisted his mouth and said, "Damned if I know. I guess we haven't spent much time on that. Maybe we'll put the egg-heads to work on it when the time comes. Zoroaster knows, we've got enough of them around now. Jed, how many think tanks have we currently got thinking?"

Jed considered for a moment before saying, "About twelve, the last time I counted. As soon as there gets to be more than twenty in one of them they split into two and start inviting new double-domes in."

Morris said, "Well, what we'll do is declare a new Constitutional Convention or something and put them to work implementing our fundamental ideas, or something like that. Maybe we'll even keep some of the old facade, like having a president. But one thing sure. We of the Triumviarate and the National Executive Committee will be the power behind the throne. We'll call the new system something like, say, Real Democracy, but *we'll* make the decisions. Most people don't really like democracy— if we ever had it— but they like to give lip service to it. What old egghead was it who said, 'Come now, the truth. Who among you would be satisfied with justice?' "

Karen said, trying to reflect, "I think you've got it wrong. I think it was Mencken and he said, 'Injustice

is relatively easy to bear; what stings is justice.'"
There came a gentle knock at the door.

Jack said, "What is it?"

A pert young woman in the suede of the Subversivettes came in and said, "Two members from Greater Washington would like to see you."

Jed growled, "We're going to have to work out some system where we don't spend our valuable time with every new member that comes along. There's thousands of them already."

But Morris said, "Show them in, uh, what's your name again, Comate?"

"Kate, Comate," she told him and stood aside for the two newcomers.

They were husky-looking specimens, wearing suede shirts and looking as though they had come out of the same pod. Both were dark of hair, dark of eye and had faces once associated with pugilists. They stood before the three National Executive Committee Members almost as though at attention.

Morris said, "Well, Comates?"

One said, "I'm Felix Bauer and this is Comate Tom Shapiro. We're both Senior Members."

"Congratulations, Comates," Jed said. "What can we do for you?"

Bauer said, "We were recruited by Dick Oppenheimer. He's an old friend of ours. Then when he came back to Greater Washington to organize a branch there, we helped him round up the necessary Candidate Members. We each got seven new recruits, making us Senior Members."

"Good work," Morris said. "How many members are there in Greater Washington now?"

"You mean, the Arlington Branch, or the Baltimore Branch?"

Karen said, "You mean there're two?"

Bauer looked at her. "'Yes, Comate. The town's too big for just one and the distances too great to work efficiently. I don't know about the Baaltimore Branch but when we left there were about 125 Full Members in the Arlington Branch and we were beginning to think in terms of spliting it and coming up with a Richmond Branch."

"Holy Jumping Zoroaster," Jed muttered.

Shapiro spoke up for the first time, saying, "We're both on GAI and there's no particular reason for us remaining in Greater Washington, so Dick suggested we move here to Center City and see if there wasn't something we could do here at the National Office."

Jack had been sizing them up thoughtfully. He said, "What did you do when you did work, or, if you never have, what were you trained for?"

Bauer said, "We owned a gym. Taught boxing, karate, that sort of thing. But practically everybody's on GAI these days and can't afford to pony up the pseudo-dollars they'd have to pay for lessons. So we had to fold. That's how we met Dick. He used to work out with us."

"I'll be damned," Jack said. "Listen, I'm head of the Minute Men. How'd you like to become captains in the Suede Shirts and be my . . . well, my bodyguards?" He added, "The pay would start at two hundred pseudo-dollars a week. More than you get on GAI."

"Well, great," Shapiro said.

Bauer said, "Sounds good to me."

Jack said, "Wizard. There's a shop right down Main Street, Number 101, that handles our uniforms. Go on down and order two with captain's insignas, and then report back here."

The two turned and hurried out.

Karen Landy looked at Jack, "What the hell," she said. "Two hundred pseudo-dollars a week for those two goons, and here I am head of the Subversivettes and general Woman Friday around here and a member of the Executive Committee to boot and all I get is one hundred and seventy-five."

Morris said, "Something new has been added. The credits are beginning to roll in. From now on, you have seven hundred and fifty a week." He thought about it. "And so does Dick Oppenheimer."

He looked around. "Since we're all here we might as well call it an executive meeting. Is there anything to be brought up?"

Jed said, "I thought of something. We're beginning to hire people for the more responsible jobs. I think we ought to request that every member make his Dossier Complete available to the Party. Not obligatory but it would be available if we wanted to secure information involving hiring new Party employees. Then if we need, say, another half dozen National Organizers we can have the computers search through all the dossiers and find those members most suited for the jobs."

"How about those members who don't voluntarily make their dossiers available to the organization?" Karen said.

"We don't give any of them jobs. A requirement for getting any job in the Party is that their dossiers are available."

"Sounds good to me," Morris said. "If everybody's in favor we'll do it."

Karen said to Jack, "What in the hell do you need with a couple of bodyguards?"

Jack said sourly, "Don't you see this black eye I'm sporting? A few nights ago three funkers took exception to my recruiting Minute Men from the local hoverbike club. They were beginning to work me over when some of the new Candidate Members came on the scene, like the Canadian Royal Mounted to the rescue, and cleaned them up. I have a sneaking suspicion that before we're through all members of the NEC will have to have at least a couple of bodyguards. We ought to be able to recruit them from the Minute Men."

"Wow," Jed said.

Morris said, "Is there anything else to come before the meeting?"

Karen said, "I thought of something we might advocate. A return to gladiator shows."

"Zoroaster," Jack muttered. "Why?"

"Several reasons," Karen said definitely. "For one, lots of people love violence. The more popular shows on Tri-Di are portraying violence of one sort or another; war, westerns, suspense, spy, detective."

"Sure," Morris said, "But where'd the gladiators come from. The Romans used to use slaves."

"Volunteers. No pay. Some crackpots would love to have the attention of being in the arena, being on Tri-Di, being celebrities in the sports magazines. If and when they got killed, wizard. Gets such drivel-happy types off the streets, keeps them from mugging honest citizens and such."

"What would our in be?" Jed said.

"The whole thing would be government run," Karen said. "All admission tickets sales would go to us."

Morris shook his head in despair. "You know,

Karen, I'm beginning to suspect that you're the most bloodthirsty mopsy I've ever met. However, all in favor say aye."

"No," all three men said in unison.

"Sissies," Karen grunted.

# 12

When Dick Oppenheimer entered the National Office he stopped for a moment in shock. The elevator banks were flanked on each side by two young men in Minute Men uniforms. The corridors were teeming with scurrying men and women, median age about thirty. All wore at least suede shirts, a considerable number were in Minute Man uniform and all of the women wore the official dress of the Subversivettes. There was a large double receptionist's desk directly across from the elevators, at which sat two bright young things offering a choice of flavors, blonde and brunette.

All in sight were obviously members of the Subversive Party save two workers in coveralls who were wheeling an impressive-looking business machine down the hall. They were being supervised by two Minute Men.

One of the elevator guards approached Dick Oppenheimer and took in his suede shirt. He said, politely enough, "May I see your Party card, Comate?"

The other's eyes became slightly suspicious. "As of last week, all Party members carry an I.D. card. It's for security purposes. We don't want any crackpots coming into the National Office, or any of the State Offices, and tossing a bomb or something."

"Good idea," Dick said. "But I've been up in Alaska and haven't even heard about it."

"Is there anyone here at the National Office who could identify you?"

"There ought to be," Dick told him, slightly irritated. "I'm the First National Organizer and a member of the National Executive Committee."

The other said hurriedly, "Yes, Comate. Sorry, Comate Oppenheimer. We were told you would be returning today. But, just to be sure, may I see your Universal Credit Card or other identification?"

Dick brought out his credit card and handed it over. "At least you boys are efficient," he said.

The other examined the card, handed it back and put his right fist over his heart. "Thank you, Comate," he said. "It's necessary. This last week we caught two funkers, both religious cranks, one with a smoke bomb and one with a gyro-jet rocket pistol."

Dick was taken aback. "You did, eh? What'd you do with them?"

"Handed them over to the police." The Minute Man cleared his throat. "Of course, we had to, uh, work them over a bit disarming them."

"Wizard," Dick said. "Carry on, Comate. I'll get a membership I.D. card soonest."

He went over to the reception desk and confronted the blonde. She put her right fist over her left breast and said, "What can I do for you, Comate?"

His every inclination was to tell her she could give him a date for that evening, with a bed in eventual mind, but instead he said, "I've been on a rather long organizing tour in Hawaii and Alaska and can see that changes have been made around here since I left. To what extent have the offices been extended?"

"We cover the whole floor now, Comate. And I understand that plans are being made to take over the floor below."

"Jumping Zoroaster. Then I imagine offices have been shuffled around a bit. How do I find Mo, that is, Morris Malone?"

"Comate Malone is in Cleveland speaking at a rally, Comate."

"Well, how about Jed Kleiser?"

"Comate Kleiser was scheduled to address the professors and students of the Havard School of Economics at lunch today. He should return this afternoon.

"And Comate Jack Zieglar?"

"He is leading a demonstration of Minute Men and others against City Hall to protest police interference with our open air meetings."

"I'll be damned. Listen, I'm the First National Organizer. Do I have a desk or something assigned to me?"

"Oh yes, Comate Oppenheimer. Your offices are down the corridor there, five down, to the left. Your name is on the door. Do you wish me to escort you?"

"That won't be necessary," he said. "Thank you, Comate."

He turned to leave and behind him could hear the blonde whisper to the brunette, her voice worshipful, "Do you know who that was? The First National Organizer. Isn't he *cute*?"

And another whisper, in return, "How would you like to date *him*?"

The first office he was about to pass had a sign on it, FELIX BAUER, and beneath that, SUBVERSIVE SECURITY. There was a tough-looking Minute Man posted to one side of it. His uniform was slightly different than that originated by Jack Zieglar. There was only one belt across the chest and he wore suede shoes, rather than boots.

Dick was about to go on when the door opened and a similarly attired man came out. Dick stared at him.

The other said quickly, "Dick! I thought you were still up in Alaska."

Dick said cautiously, "Mo and the boys suggested I come back here to the National Office. There's evidently more work for me to do here than on the road."

"Damn well told," the other said. "Come on in." He stood aside for Dick to enter.

Inside turned out to be a moderately large office with three desks occupied by three efficient looking young men, busily at paper work.

They passed on through into a larger office which contained two desks, behind the smaller of which was another brisk looking young man, also wearing the same uniform.

Felix Bauer said, "That'll be all, Lieutenant Walters. Go on over to Communications and check out how Comate Zieglar's demonstration is going. If we can provoke the police into an overt act, it'll hit national headlines."

The other came to his feet, pressed his right fist over his heart, and left.

Dick said, "What's that hand over the chest bit?"

Felix Bauer grinned. "That's a contribution of mine. The new Subversive Party salute. You know, something like Hitler's old upraised arm, or the Communist's clenched left hand held shoulder high."

Dick looked around and said, "This place couldn't possibly be bugged?"

"Not a chance," the other told him. Ken and I have checked it out with every mop in the Department of Dirty Tricks."

"What in the hell are you doing here, Pete? And what in the hell's Subversive Security?"

"Sit down, Cliff," Bauer said, walking behind the larger of the two desks and seating himself. "First of all, my Party name is Felix Bauer and Ken's is Tom Shapiro. He's my deputy. The Party is growing so fast that even the computers can hardly keep up. Most of the NEC members and even several of the State Executive Committee members have had weirdos take a crack at them in one way or the other. So, at my suggestion, we started up Subversive Security. Bodyguards, in short. Something like the United States Secret Service. I'm Commander. Tom— you're going to have to get used to our new names, don't slip up in front of any of the other SP people since supposedly we were all three good friends back in Greater Washington..."

"I'm not stupid, *Felix*," Dick said testily.

"Okay, okay, you look like a kid but you've been on this assignment longer than I have, so you rank me. At any rate, *Tom* and I are in command of Subversive Security. All of our boys have gun permits, even."

Dick looked at him for a long appraising moment. He said evenly, "Don't use them. Not at this stage of the game."

"Of course not," the other said reassuringly. "We're playing it absolutely frigid."

"How big's this Subversive Security? What a name. It sounds like a contradiction in terms. I'm surprised that Mo let it go by. The initials are SS which in Nazi times brought up quite a stench."

"What about Subversive Scouts? By the way, half the teenagers in the country seem to be joining that. We have our work cut out finding enough instructors in karate and so forth, to keep them happy. Oh, yeah, well, there's about five hundred Subversive Security men."

Dick thought about it. "How many of them are our IBI agents?"

"All of them," Bauer said, grinning. "This goddamned thing is a geometric progression. To get to be a Full Member, you have to get two new recruits..."

Dick said impatiently, "I know, I know, goddammit, Pete, please remember I was an NEC member in this outfit before you were moved in. In fact, I'm beginning to suspect I was one of the charter members."

"Okay, okay. At any rate, for an agent to be effective at all he's got to be a Full Member. That means he's got to enlist two more members. If we really want to goose him up into a useful position, he's got to be a Senior Member. This snappy-cunt Karen Landy wants to up it one rank. Centurian Member. You have to have recruited one hundred new Candidate Members. Then you automatically get some job such as State Secretary of a State Executive Committee with a nice salary."

"Is there any way of getting a drink around here? I'm getting punch drunk with all this."

Felix Bauer got up and went over to an elaborate autobar in a corner of the room and returned with two snifter glasses. He handed one to Dick Oppenheimer, who sniffed and then looked at his host.

"Zoroaster! This is real cognac."

"Yeah. We ranking executives don't do so bad.

The basic slogan is still *What's In It For Me?* I've got an unlimited expense account."

"All right. "I've been out in the boondocks, Alaska and Hawaii. What's this State Executive Committee routine?" Dick said.

"Each state now has an SEC, head by a State Secretary and with a whole bunch of committees. And each, of course, have a few Subversive Security men assigned to them."

"And you mean the whole SS, I suppose you call it, are our agents?"

"Right. The Chief figured that was the best part of the organization we could infiltrate."

Dick got up and went over to the autobar and dialed himself another brandy. He came back with it and said, "Holy smokes. Here I am, the First National Organizer and on the NEC and you're head of Subversive Security."

"I'm a member of the NEC now, too."

"You are! Holy Zoroaster, how many agents of the bureau are in this outfit now?"

"Practically all of them, Cliff. Remember, to become a Senior Member you have to have made at least seven converts altogether."

Dick Oppenheimer slumped back into his chair. "I haven't reported to the Chief for a couple of weeks or more and that was about developments in Alaska and Hawaii where they're pyramiding the same as they are here on the mainland. What does he think?"

"He thinks it's getting out of hand so rapidly that we better hit Mo Malone and possibly the other two members of the Triumvirate."

Dick goggled him. "Hit 'em! There hasn't been anything done like that since the old C.I.A. days."

"Without them, the whole damned outfit would

fall apart. Them and possibly that mopsy Karen Landy."

Dick said glumly, "It'd probably fall apart if only Mo Malone were liquidated. He's the real brains behind the organization. Have any of you boys dug out anything we can use against them?"

"There's nothing to dig out, Cliff. That's their strong point. They haven't got any secrets and don't advocate anything illegal."

"Where does all the money come from to run this place? There must be several hundred office workers out there." Disk gestured with his head in the direction of the hall from which he had just come.

"Collections at meetings, donations, but mostly the original membership five pseudo-dollars and dues. This damn organization doubles every few days. But, for that matter, it isn't as expensive to run as you'd think. There are only a handful of us on the Party payroll. Everybody else is on GAI and they donate their time for free. Whoever originally dreamed up that Guaranteed Annual Income deal probably never figured that it'd be the kiss of death for this government. The Subversive Party has potentially millions of people who can donate their full time to it."

Dick Oppenheimer finished his drink and came to his feet. "I'll have to locate my office and get organized, Felix. See you later."

He left and continued down the hall until he reached a door lettered RICHARD OPPENHEIMER and FIRST NATIONAL ORGANIZER. There was an identity screen on it and it had evidently already been keyed to his face since the door swung open on his approach.

Inside was a small reception room with a girl in

Subversivette uniform behind it. She was a red head, green of eyes, wide of mouth, perky of nose, and just slightly on the plumpish side.

She popped to her feet and put her right hand over her well rounded left breast and gushed, "Comate Oppenheimer!"

He made the same salute, feeling foolish, and said, "Call me Dick. Who are you?"

"I'm your secretary, Comate . . . Dick. My name's Betty Ann Terwilliger."

Dick looked at her appreciatively. He said, "Oh, you are, eh? I didn't know I had one."

She said, "I didn't expect you'd be quite so soon, Comate. There are some papers on your desk that need your attention. The NEC has decided that we need at least one full time organizer in each state. They'll be called State Organizers with the same duties as National Organizer; that is, they organize new branches. But there'll still be about twenty National Organizers who'll go around supervising them. You'll be in charge of selecting all of them."

"Zoroaster," Dick said, in mild complaint. He looked down at a magazine on her desk. "What's that?" It had a light suede-colored cover.

She took it up and handed it to him. "It's the first edition of the SUBVERSIVE DIGEST. It just came out today. Your wonderful article is in it, Comate . . . Dick."

"I'll be damned." He took it and headed for the inner office.

His office was approximately the size of that of Felix Bauer, the Security head. Since he had never used it, never even seen it before, it had a sterile quality. There were several steel files, which he assumed were empty, some bookshelves without books, save a few copies of the *Subversive Manifesto*, and an impressively large desk with the usual equipment; voco-typer, two phone screens and a National Data Bank library booster.

There was a small pile of letters and other papers before him when he sat down, but for the moment he ignored them and looked at the magazine in fascination. It was well presented. Evidently, the Party had acquired some top people in the publishing field.

It was full of ads. He wondered if Jed was the editor. Jed never missed a chance at picking up a quick pseudo-dollar and he wasn't beyond twisting the arm of any advertiser who was vulnerable to Party pressure. But no. To his surprise the list of editors contained the names of several writers whom he recognized. Although it was called a 'digest' most of the articles were originals and his eyes widened at the authors. It would seem that the Party was beginning to attract the intelligensia.

He came upon one page entitled CHILDREN'S SUBVERSIVE BRIGHT SAYINGS. The first one read,

*I said to my Daddy, "Daddy why do all the Democratic Republican politicians look constipated? Is it because they're full of crap?"*

# 13

Dick closed his eyes momentarily in pain and then continued to thumb through the publication. He was moderately surprised to find a photograph of himself and an article entitled SUBVERSIVE AIMS and signed *Richard Oppenheimer, First National Organizer.* It would seem that the Party had a staff of ghost writers. He read the first few inspiring paragraphs and gave it up. It was the same old Party propaganda.

One of his phone screens lit up and Karen Landy's face was there, looking a bit wide-eyed.

She said, "Dick. I wasn't sure if you were back yet or not."

He said, "Cheers, Karen. What spins?"

"Could you come over to my office? We have, uh, a distinguished visitor and none of the Triumvirate are in the National Office."

"Sure. Where's your office?"

"Your girl will show you."

Dick went out to Betty Ann and she took him out into the teeming corridor and pointed the way to Karen Landy's office.

There were two sharp looking Subversivettes flanking the door. Cute, but on the athletic looking side. They eyed him as he approached.

He said, "I'm Dick Oppenheimer. Comate Landy is expecting me."

They evidently recognized him from photographs. Both gave the Party salute and one opened the door which was lettered in suede colored letters, KAREN LANDY, DIRECTOR OF SUBVERSIVETTES.

Inside, the preliminary office was considerably larger than his own. There were four desks presided over by the same number of Subversivettes, all working away as though the office was understaffed. They didn't look up at his entry. Dick wondered vaguely if anyone knew just how large the Subversive Party was, these days. And who was handling it all. Obviously, the NEC wasn't large enough to do more than keep its fingers on the pulse. Who was making decisions, who was organizing efforts? He had heard in Hawaii that there was now a national organ, *The Subversive Press* but he had thus far never seen a copy and hadn't a clue to who was editing it. Certainly, none of the Triumvirate would have the time.

He passed on through to the sanctum sanctorum of Karen Landy.

Karen's office gave at least some lip service to femininity. The curtains were colorful, there were some paintings on the walls. There was even a vase with roses on her desk.

There was also Karen, looking fabulous in her Subversivette dress uniform and as though she had just left a beauty parlor five minutes ago.

And there was an aged stranger. He was dressed in the stiff, semi-formal clothing of an earlier age, held a cane between his legs, affected a monocle— the only one Dick had ever seen outside a Tri-Di historical show, or an old movie— and his head was either completely bald or shaven. His face was gray and expressionless.

When Dick entered, the stranger came to his feet, clicked his heels together and did a half bow.

Karen said, "Comate Oppenheimer, may I introduce Herr Baron Otto Von Zogbaum, delegate from the Neo-National Socialist Party of Common Europe?"

The Baron shot out his right arm in upraised salute. "Heil Hitler," he said.

Dick blinked, recovered, and replied with the new Subversive Party salute, hand clenched over his heart.

The Baron said, "It is the honor to meet the First National Organizer of the Zubverzive Party."

Dick looked at Karen to be clued.

She said, very earnestly, "The Baron has come from Common Europe..."

"From Chermany, actually," the Baron said. "Ven ve Neo-National Zocialists come to power we vill first disazzociate ourselves from zis Common Europe and zen..." He combed his toothbrush mustache with a thumbnail. "...und zen ve vill perhapz zee vat vill happen to them fellers that in the pazt have ztood in ze vay of the Vaterland, *nicht*?"

"Please be seated, gentlemen," Karen said.

Dick sank weakly into a leather comfort chair.

On the small table to the Baron's right was a king-size glass of dark beer.

Dick looked at Karen in pleading.

She said, "A drink, Comate?"

He said, "I'm dying on the vine."

She got up and went over to a more than usually elaborate autobar, turned to him and raised her eyebrows.

"Cognac," he said.

When she had brought it and resumed her own chair, Dick looked at their visitor.

The Baron beamed at him and said, "Berhaps you have heard of Baron Von Zogbaum? Zumtimes zey call me the last of the Nazis."

Dick took him in again. The other was an old duffer, but he didn't look old enough to be a Nazi. "A Nazi?" Dick said.

"Ja," the other said. I vas a verevolf ven I vas only twelf years old."

"Verevolf?" Karen said blankly.

"You mean werewolf?" Dick said, just as blankly.

"Ja, that is vat I said, *nicht*? Ven the *verdammen* Allies invaded the Reich, it vas decided to form an unterground, a secret resistance. Ve called ourselves verewolves."

Dick was fascinated. He had never heard of a Nazi resistence during the occupation. He said, "And how did it verk, I mean work, out?"

The German shrugged sadly. "Ve neffer got off ze ground."

Karen said carefully, "Ah, Baron Von Zogbaum, I've read quite a bit about the National Socialist Party. Tell me, after all these years, looking back, how do you feel about the Jews and, uh, I believe at the time it was called the final solution to the Jewish problem?"

"Ach, ja. Ze final zolution to the Chooish problem." He shook his head sadly. "Zere der Fuehrer made a big mistake, but zen he vas alvays too lenient... lenient you zay?... Ja, lenient. He vas too chentle, too kind hearted, *nicht*? Next time, effrybody goes."

They stared at him. "Everybody?" Karen blurted.

"Ja," the Baron nodded in satisfaction. "Choos, Polacks, niggers, wops, them Chinamens. Only Aryans will be left, Ja?"

Dick finished his brandy with one stiff-wristed motion and coughed over it.

He said, "Baron, tell me, what was your purpose in getting in touch with the Subversive Party?"

"Vell, ven ve heard of this new Bardy in America ve thought berhaps you might be kindred zpirits . . . you say kindred, *nicht?* Vishing to overthrow ze government. Zo, I vas zent to contact you. To zee if zhere might be zum vay ve could help."

"Such as what?" Dick said with caution.

"Vell, for one zing ve haff on hand a good deal of Nazi var surplus. Perhaps ve could loan you zum."

"Nazi war surplus?" Karen said.

"Ja," he told her. "Left over from ze good old days, *nicht*?"

"What kind of war surplus?" Dick said, still cautiously.

"Vell, thumbscrews, blueprintz for gas chambers, dedstical squeezers. Ach, you should hear them fellers when you tighten up ze zcrew on the dedstical squeezers."

Dick could feel his face going green. He said hurriedly, "See here, Baron Von Zogbaum, we appreciate your coming to see us and your offering of help. However, none of the members of the Triumvirate are available. You must realize the large number of trips they must make to give speeches at rallies and so forth. I suggest that for now you return to report to your organization and I'll give your message to our, uh, fuehrers and they'll get in touch. Don't call us, we'll call you."

He came to his feet, as did Karen.

The German cleared his throat, somewhat unhappily, but stood also and allowed them to escort him to the door, one on each arm. There, he clicked his heels and his right arm shot up once again.

"Heil Hitler," he said.

Karen and Dick made the Subversive Party salute. After they had closed the door behind the Baron, they both leaned their backs on it, as though fearful that he might try to return.

"Wow," Dick said.

Karen shook her head. She looked down at her wrist chronometer. "Damn," she said. "The Subversive Hour is on. We'll miss part of Ted's broadcast." She led the way back to their chairs and flicked a button on her desk to activate the Tri-Di.

"Ted who?" Dick said. "And what is this Subversive Hour thing?"

"Our Tri-Di program. Seven days a week. Ted Blacks's our commentator."

"Ted Black! Why, he's the most prestigious Tri-Dicommentator going."

"Ummm, that he is," she said. "And he's a Party member. We latched onto him between sponsors and he's being paid the same as an NEC member. In fact, he is an NEC member. He's in charge of our news media."

Ted Black's earnest face faded in.

He was saying, ". . . question has been asked what kind of a song is this *Subversion Forever . . .*"

Dick looked at Karen. "Subversion Forever?"

"It's our Party anthem. We had half the song writers in Tin Pan Alley compose it for us. Very stirring. Listen."

Ted Black was saying, looking directly, very sincerely, into lens, ". . . the idea being that we can't be serious. That surely, once the SP has come to power, we don't still want subversion. That we don't want to subvert the *new* society. That would mean it too would be changed and the leaders thrown out of office. But folks, that's exactly what the Subversive Party does mean. No socioeconomic system can remain static. Times change, new advances are made in science, in production, in our mores, in our way of life. We must continually subvert the old institutions and make room for the new."

He paused impressively, before going on. "There are no institutions so much as politico-economic ones but that must continually be reappraised. The Subversive Party makes no claim of considering itself the *last* answer. In actuality, it considers itself to be one of the first answers. Socioeconomics must change at least as fast as every other science, and human knowledge, as was pointed out by such great minds of the past as Dr. Robert Oppenheimer and Arthur C. Clarke, is doubling every eight or ten years. We cannot be confined to the political and economic theories of our grandfathers, nor, in these days of rapid progress, even by those of our fathers. The Subversive Party will continue to sing, with full heart, *Subversion Forever*!"

Dick said, "Holy Jumping Zoroaster. The program of this outfit is beginning to take on elements of seriousness."

Karen said softly, "Yes. It started off as a gag. It's rapidly becoming the hope of the nation. Did you know that since you went on your most recent organizational tour that practically every ecology, antipollution and conservationist organization in the country has come over to us lock-stock-and-barrel? They're particularly keen on our advocation that Wyoming and most of Montana be turned into a gigantic National Park where we'll bring back the buffalo, elk, antelope and other wild life, and even any Indians that wish to return to their old nomadic way of life."

"Holy smokes," Dick said.

Ted Black was saying, "And now we'll take in Comate Jack Zieglar and his Minute Men and others, peacefully marching on City Hall to protest governmental interference with the legal public open air meetings sponsored by the Subversive Party, in full accord with the traditions of free speech of this nation. Please note the full ranks of police and even armored cars which are drawn up in hopes of suppressing this peaceful demonstration."

Ted Black's face faded and the Tri-Di lenses focused in on a street scene. It was the avenue before Center City's governmental buildings. A stand had been raised before the City Hall steps and on it were Jack Zieglar and half a dozen other men in Minute Men uniform. Dick didn't recognize any of the others but their insignia ran from captain to colonel.

The lens zoomed in on the paraders. Up the street came a contingent of teenagers, about twenty abreast. The leading marchers held high a banner with the party emblem and in large type SUBVERSIVE SCOUTS and beneath that *Center City Company* and then *Troop One.*

The lenses telescoped still closer in. To one side marched a younger edition of Jack Zieglar, though there was a bit of a sullen expression to his face. He was counting cadence and it came over the air.

*Hip, two, three, four,*
  *Kick four to your left.*
*Hip, two, three, four*
  *Kick four to your left.*
*Hippity hoppity*
*Hippity hoppity*
  *Hip.*

"That's Freddy Zieglar, Jack's kid brother," Karen said, "He's National Commander of the Subversive Scouts."

"Yeah," Dick said. "He looks tougher than Jack."

"He is."

Evidently, Freddy didn't know he was on lens. He said, from the side of his mouth. "Okay, you cloddies, dress it up. Dress it up. We're coming in to the salute."

When the troop reached the reviewing stand all eyes went left, and clenched fists to the heart.

Jack and his officers returned the salute.

Another contingent of Subversive Scouts was coming up.

Dick said to Karen, "Where in the hell did they all come from?"

"We've been bussing them in since before dawn from every town with a troop of scouts within a hundred miles. I should be up on the stand with Jack to take the salute of my Subversivettes when they pass. But somebody had to hold the fort here at the National Office."

The scouts went by, troop after troop, seemingly endless.

Next were at least several hundred suede-shirted young men and women. They bore a banner, STUDENTS FOR SUBVERSION, and they too saluted as they passed the reviewing stand, albeit somewhat more raggedly than had the scouts.

Karen said, as though in passing, "The mayor refused permission for the demonstration."

"He did?" Dick blurted. "Then . . ."

Just then the Tri-Di lenses left the parade momentarily and focused in on a police officer who stood on the curb, a police riot baton in his right hand. About five feet down from him stood another policeman, similarly equipped. The faces of both were wan.

Karen said, "Last night, they brought in elements of the National Guard. From what we hear, they're encamped on the outskirts of town. And, from what we hear, they're refusing orders to enter Center City. Half of them are said to be Party members, including the officers. We've got a squad of soap box orators out there haranguing them, trying to get them to join the parade, but so far without luck."

"Holy Jumping Zoroaster," Dick muttered.

A contingent of suede-colored hoverbikes began to pass, and the Tri-Di lenses focused back on them.

Karen reached out and switched off the set. She said, "If I've seen Jack's Minute Men demonstrating once, I've seen them a hundred times. What in the name of Zoroaster is it about men that they like to parade?"

"Damned if I know," Dick said. "How many men do we have in the Minute Men now?"

"Who knows? The figures go up daily. There's over eighteen thousand in the Hoverbike Corps alone."

She looked at her wrist chronometer and said, "I've been at this damned desk for something like fifteen hours. What do you say we go up to my apartment and I'll bring you up to date on developments here at the National Office since you've been away."

"Wizard. Sounds good to me," he said. "What do you mean, *up* to your apartment?"

She stood and stretched mightily, the way a man stretches rather than an ultra-feminine woman.

She said, "We've all got apartments on the top floor. Saves time and is handy for security."

# 14

Dick Oppenheimer followed her out into the corridor and to an elevator off to one side of the ordinary banks.

There were two impressively bulky Minute Men posted there. On spotting Karen, they immediately saluted, but they gave Dick a quick once over.

Karen said, "Jim, Bill, this is Comate Oppenheimer, the First National Organizer. He's just gotten back from an extended tour and will be in residence from now on."

They both saluted again.

In the elevator, Karen said, "This is a private deal, going to the penthouse and terrace apartments."

"What's all this security curd?" Dick said.

"Necessary," she told him. "They're beginning to try and crack down on us. At the beginning the government and the Democratic Republican Party gave us the silent treatment. Probably hoping we'd just go away. They did what they could to keep us out of the news media. The police wouldn't give us permits for open air meetings, Party picnics in the parks to raise money, parades and so forth. We didn't mind too much then. If you hold some supposedly mass activity and only a couple of hundred people show up then it shows your weakness. But when you build up to having thousands, it's another thing. That demonstration that you just witnessed, Jack's march on City Hall, is an example. We're so large now that they can't crack down. We've even got a contingent in the local police and its organization is rapidly becoming national."

"I imagine they call themselves the Subversive Police," Dick said smiling.

"Of course," she said.

He looked upward in plea to such powers as might be.

She said, "At any rate, they're beginning to run scared. And we don't know how long it might be before they start resorting to strongarm methods. So we have our Subversive Security organization."

The elevator slowed to a halt.

They emerged into as posh a hallway as Dick Oppenheimer had ever seen. There was a Minute Man posted at the elevator, and he saluted them.

Karen said, "Lefty, this is Comate Oppenheimer, the First National Organizer. He's in Apartment AA."

She led the way. "I'm down here."

Dick said, "What's this Apartment AA stuff?"

"All top officials are up here now. These are terrace apartments. Mo, Jack and Jed have the three penthouses, the aristocratic sons of bitches."

Dick whistled softly between his teeth.

Karen shrugged. "To the victors belong the spoils, or whatever the saying is. What's in it for me, for short."

Dick shook his head and said, "Have we upped our salaries?"

"Why should we?" She shrugged again as the identity screen of Apartment DD recognized her and the door opened before them. "All members of the National Executive Committee are on unlimited expense accounts. If our salaries were too high, some muckracker might pick up the fact and reveal to the country that the leadership of the Subversive Party is making a good thing of it for themselves."

The apartment beyond was hardly Spartan. Dick did another almost silent whistle.

She led the way into a sunken living room and tossed her bag to a cocktail table and headed for the autobar.

"What'll you have? she said, back over her shoulder. "I've got some wonderful prehistoric Scotch."

"I'll have some wonderful prehistoric Scotch," he said. "You mean your autobar isn't hooked into the regular building facilities?

"Hell, no," she told him. "We members of the NEC have our own special supply. None of this ersatz guzzle for us."

He sank down onto a couch and waited for her to join him with the drinks.

She came back and handed him his and then settled down a few feet from him on the couch. He sipped. She had been right, it was wonderful Scotch and undoubtedly prehistoric. It was water color, as vodka or gin, but its aroma was pure Scotch.

He said, "How come no color?"

"Unblended Scotch comes this way. The color you're used to is added when it's blended. The Scots practically never export the unblended product. This is it."

"I learn something every day," he said, taking another sip. It was the smoothest guzzle he'd ever drunk. She hadn't even added ice or water. You sipped this as you did a liqueur.

"All right," he said. "Bring me up to date. I've been getting regular reports from Mo or Jed, but sometimes I've been too busy to read them."

"Let's see. Since you were here last, the *Subversive Manifesto* has become a run away best seller of all time. Except for the Bible there's never been a bigger one. It's already been translated into nineteen languages and foreign equivalents of the Subversive Party are beginning to form. There's going to be an International Convention along in here somewhere. We already have fraternal connections with some of them, but there's nothing definite as yet. World Government is the supposed eventual goal."

"Wow," he said.

"And, let's see. Ernest Faulkner, the best selling novelist, has joined up and his new book is to be contributed to the Party. It's a novel but it deals with the disintegration of modern society and the need for a new socioeconomic system to replace it. Several other pro-Party books are also being written. We've got quite a few writers now. I'm too busy with the Subversivettes to keep up with it all. We've also got a passle of Party hack writers on the payroll who are busily churning out pamphlets and brochures by the dozen, on things like pollution, planned obsolescence, adulteration of food, the high price of medicines that cost a fraction of what you pay for them to be manufactured. Things like hearing aides that are manufactured for $25 and sell for over $400. Stuff like that. Anti-war pamphlets, anti-military-industrial combines. And, oh yes, a lot of material on corruption in present day politics, that goes right up as far as the White House. We've got a real genius of a muckraker on that one. Vivid descriptions of the President's homes in Hawaii, Acapulco, the Bahamas— all at the public expense."

Dick took another whack at his whiskey. "To get back to this Democratic Republicans no longer ignoring us, trying to pretend we don't exist..."

She laughed, and on Karen laughter looked good. She said, "Like I said, at first they gave us the silent treatment but then they woke up to the fact that the people were taking us to their breasts until said titties were worn to nubbins. Then they got out their party hacks and began giving speeches all over the country, and attacking us on Tri-Di, especially in the cities where we're the strongest. Actually, it just plays into our hands."

He scowled at her. "How do you mean? Frankly, our jerry-built program has a lot of knockable stuff in it."

"Well, the NEC has sent out orders to all branches to attend these hall meetings and lectures of the Democratic Republicans, in uniform if you're a Subversivette or Minute Man, or, at least, in suede shirts. Subversive Scouts stand outside and hand out our leaflets, saying snide things such as, 'Here you are, folks. Something interesting to read while the lecture is going on.

"Other Party members set up stands displaying our pamphlets and the *Subversive Manifesto* and do a land office business selling our material to the very audiences that the Democratic Republicans are attempting to appeal to."

"Zoroaster! Don't we get any physical response to those tactics?"

"Sometimes. But usually the bully-boys in the opposite camp take one look at our Minute Men and Subversive Scouts and decide to be discreet."

She went on. "Inside, at these lectures, orders are

strict. There is to be no heckling. Instead, every time the speaker makes a point, or even a minor point, all SP members are to laugh and the louder, the better. If by any chance any SP member is arrested they are to submit instantly without any controversy whatsoever. Down at police headquarters, every station house in town, are representatives of the Subversive Liberties Union..."

"The what!" Dick ejaculated.

"Party members who are lawyers. We have a special fund for bail. Any Party member arrested is immediately bailed out. And our lawyers go to work with a vengeance, whole staffs of them. It's very seldom a member is found guilty of anything but if he is, the Party pays the fine."

"Suppose he's sentenced to jail?"

"For what? Littering the sidewalks with leaflets? Blocking the sidewalk? Giving a speech without a permit? You might fine people for such offenses, but you don't jail them. Even fines attract such attention in the news media that the judges our people are brought before are taking it easy. And very often we'll fight a hundred dollar fine right up to the Supreme Court, milking it for publicity all the way.

"Sometimes the cops try to get cute. In Baltimore, the local branch was holding an open air meeting in Druid Hill Park. The police came in force and arrested the whole bunch, over a hundred members, and a bunch of potential Candidate Members as well, and hauled them off to the slammer. They figured that with that many we couldn't possibly pay all the bail. Our treasury, of course, is a national one. The Subversives Liberties Union had them all out within an hour. You can imagine the reaction. All those who weren't already members, immediately joined up and some gave considerable donations in view of their indignation."

Dick shook his head. "The way it's going, you can't be out of town more than a couple of weeks before being completely out of step. Where's it going to end, Karen? It started out with three bored men on GAI who dreamed up a scheme to sucker their fellow men into a new party and getting a rake-off selling them suede shirts."

She got up to renew their drinks and said, once again over her shoulder, "We're going to win, Dick. It sounds fantastic, but I'm beginning to believe that we're going to take the next election."

"The *next* election. Holy Zoroaster, Karen, that's not as far away as all that. The *next* election. We've never contested an election. We don't know the first thing about it."

"We'll learn," she said, bringing back the fresh drinks and smirking at him.

He was flabbergasted. "Those Democratic Republicans are old hands at politics. They know all the ropes from a couple of centuries back. They'll do everything from stuffing ballot boxes to miscounting our votes."

Karen said evenly, "Dick, you don't change the temperature by fiddling with the thermometer. When the majority of the American people, particularly an overwhelming majority, want a change, they'll get it— stuffed ballot boxes or no."

He was scowling once more. "I can't imagine them giving up without a fight. Didn't one of the old revolutionists, Karl Marx or somebody, once say that no ruling class ever freely gave up its position of power? It has to be taken from them."

Karen tapped her mouth with the back of her

hand, stiffling a yawn. She said, "They aren't giving up their power freely, we're taking it from them. We have them by the *dedsticals,* as Baron Von Zogbaum called them, and they're beginning to feel the squeeze."

Dick flinched at that one.

She said, "Listen, do you or do you not want to take me to bed? I can understand that you might be on the tired side."

"What?"

"You heard me."

"I... why it never occurred to me. I... I thought you were Mo's girl."

"Well, think again. I'm nobody's girl except my own. And never will be. I've killed a few nights with Mo, but he has no ring in my nose, nor do I have one in his. So, do you or don't you?"

"I do," he said. He grunted and said, "I feel like I'm taking wedding vows. Either that, or that this is the first time in my life that *I've* ever been seduced."

"I doubt it," she said, grinning and coming to her feet. "You underestimate some of us mopsies. This way, lover."

He followed her into the elaborate bedroom.

"You know," he said, "in actuality, from the first time I saw you..."

"I know," she said. "And many a time since. In fact, you sometimes panted."

"I did not," he said indignantly. "I'm a gentleman and scholar of the old school."

"What does that mean?" she said, beginning to strip out of her Subversivette uniform.

"I never get an erection in public."

"Hmmm," she said, grinning wickedly at him. "I hope you do in private."

"I'll make you eat those words," he said, removing his jacket and starting to pull out his suede shirt.

"Oh, perversions, eh? I know some of my own." She was down to briefs, her fine breasts swinging free. She picked up an old coin from the bedside table. "What do you take, head or tail?"

"I was interested in tail. Wasn't that the idea?" he said in mock aggrievement.

She flipped the coin a couple of times, catching it, and said, "You call it. If you win, you're the aggressor. If I win, I am."

"Come again?" he said.

She explained to him, as she once had to Morris Malone, the whys and wherefores of the sexual act so far as being the aggressor was concerned.

He said, fascinated, standing nude now, "You mean that you take the initiative instead of me?"

"Right as rain, lover. Heads or tails?"

He said, "Heads."

She flipped the coin onto the bed and then stared down at it. "I'll be damned," she said. "Heads. So you're the boss."

## 15

In the morning, when he awoke, it was to find her, her hair dishevelled, her make up gone with the snows of yesteryear, looking at him from the pillow beside him with wide eyes.

"Good morning, Clifford," she said softly.

His own eyes narrowed. "The name is Richard," he said. "Dick to my friends."

"I sometimes wonder how many real friends people who hold down jobs like yours have. Your name is Clifford, or is it Cliff to your friends, Clifford Dix?"

"You're not making much sense."

She yawned prettily, stretched and said, "Cliff Dix of the Inter-Continental Bureau of Investigation, and one of Walter Hardenberg's hatchetmen assigned to infiltrating the Subversive Party."

He said tightly, "Where do you think you got that information?"

And she said sweetly, "You simply have no idea how the Subversive Party has spread, darling. For instance, one of the top executives of the National Data Banks is a member of the Subversivettes. Just for fun and games, I checked out the Dossiers Complete of all of our ranking officials. Surprise, surprise. That of Comate Richard Oppenheimer was a fake. And a rather clumsy one, to my amazement.

So, continuing the fun and games, I checked the dossiers of the first two Candidate Members Comate Oppenheimer brought into the Party so that he could become a Full Member. Surprise, surprise. Felix Bauer and Tom Shapiro were also IBI agents, name of Peter Twombly and Kenneth Smith, or Pete and Ken, for short. So then I checked out the five Candidate Members you proposed so that you could become a Senior Member. By this time, I was overwhelmed with surprises. All five, if we're not mistaken, were members of the IBI. Where in the name of the Holy Jumping Zoroaster do you get such numbers of IBI agents?"

Cliff said wearily, "So you told Mo and the others?"

She arched her eyebrows in mock surprise. "Why? You've been doing a wonderful job."

He stared at her as though she was completely out of her mind. "But I'm the First National Organizer and a member of the NEC."

"There's no Party rule against IBI agents being members. The dues are welcome." She yawned again. "And you've been doing an excellent job. I can see why, obviously. To keep your cover, you had to be efficient for the cause. So did Pete and Ken. They've made wonderful Subversive Security men. Why not? They're trained for that sort of thing. The SP has the most highly trained security men in the country. Practically all from the IBI."

He was still staring at her. "You can't be serious. You're telling me I'm a government agent and you don't give a damn. You even go to bed with me."

She looked at him. "You forget the Party's basic slogan, Cliff. What's in it for me? Take a look around you. There's plenty in it for me. And there's going to be more. Any revolutionist who wants to wear a hair shirt is not only drivel-happy but probably a lousy revolutionist. All right, I'm a great advocate of *What's In It For Me?* So far, there's been a lot. But what's in it for you? I doubt very much that your IBI agent pay is nearly as high as you get as First National Organizer."

He said sourly, "You know, not even the members of the Triumvirate are exactly snowy white. I happen to know Jack Zieglar took a five thousand pseudo-dollar bribe to report the inner workings of the Party to a man named Bing."

She smiled prettily and said, "You're behind the time, darling. That was the *first* time any of the NEC was approached by outsiders wanting inside information. Jack transferred the five thousand to the Party treasury. Since then, we've all been approached. I'm surprised that you haven't. I suppose it's because you've been on the move too much. Mo hit the jackpot. The Soviet Complex has him on the payroll for fifty thousand a year."

He stared at her. "What does he report to them?"

"What can he report to them? There's nothing to report that doesn't come out in our newspapers or Tri-Di broadcasts. What in the hell do you report to your boss, Hardenberg?"

"Precious little," he admitted. "You'll probably never believe me, but I was going to tell the Triumvirate myself that I was an IBI agent. I've actually finally come around to support the organization."

"Wizard," she said. "Everybody else and his cousin is coming around, why shouldn't you?" She thought about it. Finally she said, slowly, "However, you know, I'd keep it under my hat for awhile. Don't reveal to anybody else that you're an IBI man, especially don't reveal to Felix Bauer and Tom Shapiro that you've had a change in mind."

"Why not?"

"So that you can act as a double agent, in the good old cloak and dagger tradition. I don't trust your boy, Hardenberg. He's tough as nails and as ruthless as they come. When he sees that fair means— or comparatively fair— aren't working, he might try something foul. He might come up with some dirty trick."

Dick didn't like that. "Such as what?"

"How would I know? Suppose he came up with a scheme to stage an atrocity? To have some of his agents who are members of the Minute Men heave a bomb into some Democratic Republican meeting, and killing and wounding a couple of dozen people. It'd turn the country against the Subversive Party overnight."

"Holy Zoroaster, Karen. Come *on*."

"I didn't say that's what he'd pull. But if he did come up with some dirty trick, he'd probably contact you about it. You were his original agent, way back when there was only a handful of members."

"I'll think about it."

She said, "What I just mentioned isn't entirely without precedent. Did you ever read of the Haymarket Affair in Chicago back in the 19th Century? A bunch of anarchists were holding a peaceful street meeting. Hundreds of police turned up to be sure it didn't get out of hand. Somebody threw a bomb and several of the police were killed. The anarchist leaders were arrested, brought to trial and executed. Damn few honest investigators of the affair thought the anarchists guilty. Much the same happened to Tom Moony, the labor leader, also convicted of throwing a bomb at a parade. He got life in prison and wasn't pardoned for about thirty years."

"All right," Cliff Dix said, swinging his legs over the side of the bed and to the floor. "I'll admit that the fear of losing power could make some of the establishment pretty desperate."

He began to dress. "I'd better take a look at my apartment and get organized. I assume that all of the boys will be here today."

"They should be."

When he was dressed, something came to him. He brought his electronic mop from an inner pocket and looked over at her. Karen was still in bed. He put a finger to his lips in the universal gesture for silence.

She frowned at him and began to say something but then shut up, as ordered.

He activated the mop and began checking out the room. When he got near the phone screen at the side of her bed, the gadget began to hum.

He looked at her, his eyebrows high. She was bug-eyeing him and then the phone screen.

He took the mop into the living room and found that the bug there was in a floor lamp. He went into her study. The bug there, too, was planted in her desk phone screen. Three in all. There weren't any others in the apartment.

Dick Oppenheimer put the mop away and went back into the bedroom. She was still in bed, blinking rapidly in thought.

He leaned over her and put his lips against her ear and whispered, "Your apartment is bugged. Bedroom, living room, study. Don't talk it over with any of the rest until the room you're in is checked."

She nodded.

He stood up and said, "So long, Karen. See you later. Thanks for the best go round I can off hand ever remember having."

"Thank you, kind sir. It was a pleasure."

He turned and left.

He didn't have any difficulty finding Apartment AA. The layout was similar to Karen's, but the decoration was masculine. To his surprise, he found that someone had brought all of his things from his old apartment.

Following breakfast, he brought out his electronic mop again and checked out his own apartment. And, yes, it too was bugged. He wondered why, briefly, but then decided that the bugs hadn't necessarily been placed by the Inter-Continental Bureau of Investigation. They might be the work of some other government department, or even the Center City police, who didn't know of his assignment. For that matter, they might be bugs for Hardenberg, who might be interested in taping every conversation in which any member of the NEC or the Triumvirate participated.

There was another angle. If the IBI had done the bugging and if Mo or one of the others had found that their apartments were bugged, then it would look strange to them if the apartments of Dick Oppenheimer, Felix Bauer and Tom Shapiro were without them.

Theoretically, it was illegal to bug in the United States—but that was in theory.

He went into his study, locked the door behind him, and then opened a small pocket knife. One of the blades was a screwdriver. He tipped the phone screen over, unscrewed the four screws that held on the base, located the bug and deactivated it, then screwed the base back on and righted the phone.

He took out his special transceiver and set it up, leaning it against the voco-typer, and pressed its stud.

He said carefully, "Agent Clifford Dix, calling Director Walter Hardenberg. Clifford Dix, calling Walter Hardenberg. Come in, sir."

The small screen lit up and Hardenberg was there. He was as usual, brisk. He said, "Let's have your report, Dix."

Cliff Dix said, "My cover's been blown sky-high, Chief. For that matter, so have those of Peter Twombly and Kenneth Smith."

"*What!* I thought that all three of you were right at the top, confound it."

"We were. Evidently, somebody in the Bureau has been sloppy. When first I, and then Pete Twombly and Ken Smith, were given this assignment, you had somebody set up phony Dossiers Complete for us in the National Data Banks. Wizard. At that time we didn't know how far this Subversive Party was going to go. However, it snowballed and among other places from which high ranking people have enrolled are the National Data Banks. Karen Landy is no fool. I keep reporting to you that none of these people are fools. One of her Subversivettes is high-ranking in the data banks. She was given the chore of checking out the Dossiers Complete of all the ranking Subversive Party officers; NEC members, State Secretaries, National Organizers, heads of such outfits as the Subversive Scouts, Subversive Security, the Subversive Liberties Union, I suppose, and all and all. When she got to me, she found that a sloppy job had been done on my revised Dossier Complete, and evidently they ran down my real dossier."

"I'll fire that stupid funker," Hardenberg blurted, his lips tight in rage.

Clifford Dix went on. "She evidently reported it to Karen Landy. I repeat, this woman is no fool. She had her in at the National Data Banks check out first my two original Candidate Members, Felix Bauer and Thomas Shapiro. She found that their Dossiers Complete were also full of holes and ran down their real ones. Then she went to work on all the other Candidate Members all of us have recruited—at least I assume she has. The fat's in the fire, Chief."

"She's exposed you?"

Dix shook his head and his expression revealed his surprise. "Not so far as I know. She seems to think I've been doing a good job and doesn't give a damn that I'm an IBI agent."

His boss squinted at him, as though he'd gone around the corner. "You must be joking."

Cliff shook his head again. "Maybe she is, but I'm not. What it works out to is that Karen Landy, and probably the Triumvirate as well, doesn't give a hoot if the IBI joins up in the Subversive Party or not. They simply don't have any secrets. If you, yourself, came here to the National Office and questioned them, they'd answer every question— honestly."

"You must be drivel-happy!"

"Well, I'm not, sir. You've got to remember, Chief, I was practically a charter member of this far-out organization. They simply don't give a shit. And in a way that makes them invulnerable. What's the old adage? You can't cheat an honest man. And in their own slap-happy way, they're honest. They make no bones about how they stand. *What's In It For Me?* is their slogan and they cheerily tell their membership it is and invite the membership to adopt the same slogan. The whole damn Party is out to get what they can."

His superior closed his eyes for a moment before saying, "The President and his aides are up in the air. They're snorting. Even my job is shaky. What's your final summing up of Alaska and Hawaii?"

Dick said, "My estimation is that every damn Eskimo and unemployed pineapple picker in both states will be in the Party before the month is out."

"Holy Zoroaster, Dix, you were put in there to infiltrate that bunch of crackpots, not to recruit new ones!"

"That's what I've been telling you right alone," Dick said. "You don't have to recruit them, and there's no way of stopping it. This Morris Malone is a goddamned genius. He dreamed up that method of every member having to get at least two more, and eventually, seven more. That's worse than a geometric progression."

His boss sighed and his face became coldly empty. He said, wearily, "All right, Dix. Check it out with Twombly. He has my orders. This will simply speed it up a bit. We've got to take more immediate action than I had planned upon."

His face faded and Dick Oppenheimer looked at the transceiver screen for a long moment before switching the device off. Then he came wearily to his feet. This was the most screwed up mess he had ever been in in his life.

It was still early but for a long moment he looked at the autobar. The hell with it. He was going to need his brains.

He breathed deeply for a couple of minutes and

then headed for the door. He went out into the corridor and down to the Minute Man guard who stood at the special elevator.

The other saluted and Dick returned it. He said, "Does Comate Bauer have an apartment on this floor?"

"Yes, Comate. Apartment FF. It is shared with Deputy Shapiro."

"Wizard. Where is it?"

The Minute Man directed him.

Dick Oppenheimer stood before the Identity Screen and said, "Richard Oppenheimer to see Felix Bauer."

The door opened immediately and very shortly Pete Twombly came out. He had obviously just been brushing his teeth and was still in pajamas.

He said, "Cheers, Dick, what spins?"

Cliff Dix had never liked the man, though he had worked with him on several assignments. He was one of those who did the jobs that shouldn't be done, one way or the other. He was noted for chopping down politicians in far lands that the powers that be thought needed chopping down. Sometimes it turned out that the wrong side had been chopped. Sometimes he, or one of his close associates, such as Shapiro, were sent in to switch around, and chop those for whom they had been chopping earlier. It wasn't the happiest section of the Bureau to be in, but one that Cliff Dix had largely blinded himself to. He wasn't on the level that set policy. He had just been a kid when earlier agencies and bureaus had been doing things in Cuba and Chile that later made a stink.

Dick Oppenheimer said, "I've just been reporting to the Chief. Everything's fucked up."

Felix Bauer looked at him quizzically, then turned and led the way back into the living room and through it to the kitchenette. The apartment was a duplicate of Dick's.

He got coffee for them both and then said, "Like what?"

Dick sat down at the small table and said, "Our cover's been blown."

"By who?"

"Karen. I slept with her last night. I gave her a cover-up story but she's not stupid."

Bauer said, "What kind of a cover-up story?"

"I admitted I was an IBI agent, but then told her I'd been converted to the Party and was now a faithful member. She knows you're IBI too. And Ken."

Bauer said, "Actually, we already knew about this, Cliff."

"Knew about what?" Dick said, frowning. "Damn it, give me some more of that coffee."

Felix came up with the coffee. He said, "We've got them all bugged. Everything is being monitored, including your siege with The Landy last night."

"Oh, wizard. Save me my blushes."

"Don't bother. That mopsy has slept with everybody on the NEC except me."

"What's wrong with you?"

"Damned if I know."

"Maybe she thinks you don't like girls."

Bauer said dangerously, "Don't be stute, Dix."

"Oh hell, I was just trying to be funny."

"Well, don't try too hard. What's this curd about you being converted to the Party?"

Dick eyed him in disgust. "What in the hell would you expect me to tell her? I had to cover up as fast as I could."

The other thought about it before saying, "Yeah, well this has brought the whole thing to a head. Did the Chief tell you? We're going to have to set them all up and hit them."

"Holy Zoroaster, don't be drivel-happy."

"I'm in charge, Dix. You've been away."

"Damn it, that's not important," Dick said impatiently. "The thing is, you'll make martyrs out of them! The whole stupid crew."

Kenneth Smith, alias Tom Shapiro, entered from an inner room. He said, "Hi, Cliff. What spins?"

"Everything, goddammit. I was just telling Pete that our cover's been blown. He already knew it, of course."

Tom Shapiro grinned at him. "Yeah. Holy Zoroaster, that was quite a show you put on last night, Cliff."

"Shut up."

Shapiro looked at Felix Bauer. "I've just been talking to the old man. He says we can't afford to wait. He says to pull it today."

"Yeah, we'll have to," Bauer growled. He looked at Dick. "It's already been planned. The Triumvirate will all be here today. Undoubtedly, Mo Malone will call for a meeting of the NEC. We still use the original conference room for NEC meetings. There're four doors into it. Standard procedure is to have two of our Subversive Security men at each door. When everybody's present and the meeting's begun I'll signal them and they'll pop in and the shootout begins. We hit the whole Triumvirate."

"How about Karen Landy?" Dick said, in disgust at the whole situation.

"She has to go too. Too bad, but there's no alternative. We can't have any survivors as witnesses."

"How about Ted Black? Somebody said he was on the NEC now."

"Black doesn't live here. He's kept his house on the other side of town. He's got two of our Subversive Security men with him at all times. On his way over, there'll be an accident to his hovercar so that he won't make it to the meeting. He's not important. We can afford to let him go."

"I still say we'll just be making martyrs of them."

"Not the way we've got it staged. You and I will be the sole remaining NEC members of the Subversive Party, except for Black. Our story will be that Jack Zieglar was trying to put over a Party coup. That he planned to use his Minute Men and become supreme head of the Party. All of our boys, of course, will bear us out. We'll claim that Jack started the shooting and the guards burst in and nailed him, but that he had finished off Kleiser, Landy and Malone first. We'll plant a gun on Jack."

Dick thought about it, still unhappy. "Then what do we do?"

"Then we elected Tom Shapiro, here, to the NEC and a couple of the other agents in the Subversive Security. Then we go to work on this organization like Grant went to work on Richmond."

"Such as what?"

"Well, suppose we pass a rule that every Party member is assessed one hundred pseudo-dollars?"

Shapiro laughed and said, "They'd drop out of the Party like dandruff."

Dick licked his lower lip and stared up at the ceiling. He said slowly, "You know, it might work at that. It'll cause one hell of a stink. But it might work. It's not the first time there's been a so-called palace revolution in a radical outfit. Danton, Robespierre, all those French revolutionists. One by one they guillotined each other."

"Sure it'll work," Bauer said.

"And the Chief okayed it, eh?"

"That's right. In fact, he made most of it up."

Dick sighed. "All right. You boys got an extra shooter? I'd better be heeled too, just in case a wheel comes off. I don't know about Mo and Jed, but Jack was in the army and it's just possible that he packs a gun."

Shapiro got up from the chair he'd been sitting in and went over to a desk, unlocked a drawer and came up with a gyro-jet rocket pistol. He brought it over and handed it to Dick. Dick released the magazine and checked it, then thrust it back into the gun's butt and jacked a cartridge into the barrel. He set the safety and tucked the gun into his belt.

"All right," he sighed. "Can't you figure out any way we can let Karen off the hook?"

Bauer shook his head. "As head of the Subversivettes she always attends meetings. If we tried to keep her away from this one, she'd smell a rat."

Dick stood. "All right," he said again. "I'll go on back to my apartment until Mo summons us to the meeting."

## 16

When Dick Oppenheimer approached the conference room he found two men in the uniform of Subversive Security posted outside the door. He didn't recognize either of them, but one winked very slightly as they both gave the Party salute.

Dick nodded and went on through.

Malone was already there, seated at the conference table's end and writing on a pad of paper. Jack was seated two chairs down from him and looking bemused, or hungover.

In a chair, up against the wall, was a seventeen-year-old in the uniform of a Subversive Scout. Dick looked at him. It was Freddy Zieglar, that younger edition of Jack, but with his surly, tough expression.

Jack said, "Freddy thought he'd like to sit in on a few sessions of the National Executive Committee. It won't be long before he's old enough to be a Full Member and he thinks he's ambitious."

Felix Bauer and Tom Shapiro entered and Bauer, as a member of the NEC, took a place at the table across from Jack. Tom Shapiro, as Bauer's deputy, took a chair back against the wall behind his chief.

Dick sat down next to Jack, caught Bauer's eye and made a slight gesture with his head in the direction of Freddy. Bauer shrugged slightly as though indicating that there was nothing they could do about it.

Karen entered and looked around before taking her customary seat. She said, "Everybody here but Ted Black and Jed?"

Jack said, "Ted phoned. He's had an accident and the police picked him up and took him in."

Karen frowned and said, "Are our lawyers alerted?"

Jack shook his head. "It hasn't anything to do with the Party. Ted'll have to work it out on his own. It's all right. Nobody hurt."

Jed came in with a sheaf of papers in hand, as usual, tossed them to the table before his usual chair and sat down. He looked at Malone and said, "What're you doing, Mo?"

"Writing a poem," Morris said and looked up. "I guess we're all here. Let's get the show on the road. First item of business is the coming election. We're going to have to contest it."

Jed said, in protest, "Holy Zoroaster, Mo. We haven't got the time to organize a convention and choose candidates."

"We're not going to have a convention."

All eyes were on him.

"You've got to have a convention to make nominations, if you're going to put up candidates," Karen said. "Anybody knows that."

"No you don't," Morris Malone told her. "That was the old way and it was inefficient as hell, and as corrupt as hell. A handful of big shots actually decided who the candidates would be— the old smoke filled room routine— and the supposed delegates rubber-stamped their selections."

Jack said, "Wizard, but, well, isn't that more or less what we'd do?"

Morris looked at him and shook his head. "No. We're coming up with something better. We're going to locate the best men in the country to hold down national offices and, once elected and in them, to hold the new Constitutional Convention to compile a new Constitution."

Felix Bauer said, "Wizard, but how are we going to locate them?"

Morris Malone said, "I've been figuring it out. What we'll do is put the Dossiers Complete of all Party members who would like to take office into the computers. They'll select the candidates based on I.Q., ability quotient, education, experience and so forth. Those are the ones we'll nominate. They won't necessarily be handsome, good public speakers, have a good Tri-Di presence, or be able to shake hands heartily. They'll just be the best people in the country to hold down national office. And they'll sweep in. The country's fed up with the old-style politicians. According to Jed's latest figures we'd win even if the election took place tomorrow. By the time it does take place, it'll be a landslide."

"How are we going to control these jokers we get elected, when they get around to this new Constitutional Convention?" Jack said.

Morris Malone took up the sheet of paper he had been writing on and read:

"*QUIS CUSTODIET IPSOS CUSTODES?*"

Bauer scowled. "What the hell's that supposed to mean?"

Morris said, "It's from the Roman writer, Juvenal. Roughly it means— who's to be the custodians of the custodians? Here's my poem." He read:

*Who's to watch over the watchers,*
*Those who would carry the lashes?*
*What was the tune that Joshua played?*
*Who hauls the janitor's ashes?*

The rest of them looked at him with varying expressions.

Morris said, "Three unanswerable questions." And then, after taking a deep breath, "*We're* not going to come to power. The Subversive Party is, but not we of the Triumvirate nor of the NEC."

Karen said, "Have you gone drivel-happy, Mo? What the hell have we been doing all this for?"

He looked at her and there was tiredness in his face. He said, "Karen, after a socioeconomic change has been successfully pulled off, the successful revolutionists are usually a hindrance to those who come afterward and have to actually build and run the new society. Look at Tom Paine and Sam Adams in America. They were an embarassment to men like Tom Jefferson and James Madison who took up the reins after the American Revolution was won. Look at Robespierre, Danton and Marat, the big three of the French Revolution. All were killed. Look at Lenin and Trotsky. They were only in the way of Stalin and his crowd. If Lenin hadn't died when he did, Stalin probably would have done him in, just as he did the other Old Bolsheviks, Trotsky, Zinoviev, Rykov, Kamenev, Radek and so forth."

He looked around at them, one by one, including Freddy seated against the wall.

He shook his head. "We don't have the ability to run this country nor to devise a new Constitution. We did a good job of gathering the forces to improve the nation, but we can't run it. So the first thing we do, when the election has been won, is step down. We won't hurt any. A grateful country will see that we're taken care of."

Jack grunted and said, "At least nobody will be coming for us to shoot us. I think I'll retire to Switzerland. They've got good guzzle there."

Karen said, "Okay, you've sold me, Mo. I vote yes. I think I'll move to Switzerland too. They've got some of the best looking men in the world there."

Jed said, "Yeah. We'll sweep the elections all right, and then step down. Hell, I wouldn't want to try and run the country even if I could. Too much work. And Mo's right, I couldn't and neither could the rest of you. Switzerland sounds good to me. I'll write my memoirs."

Felix Shapiro brought forth his transceiver, saying, "I think you're right, too. You would win the election. However, nobody's going to Switzerland, or anywhere else." He activated the communications gadget and said into it, "All right, boys, come on in."

There were sounds of scuffling out in the halls, shouts and banging.

Freddy shot to his feet.

Felix Bauer and Tom Shapiro stood as well, both of them with astonishment on their faces. Their hands shot beneath their jackets.

But Dick Oppenheimer had them covered. He had long since brought his gyro-jet rocket pistol from his belt and been holding it in his lap.

He snapped, "Don't bother to draw, you two. I'll blast you half way through the wall."

The doors, all four of them, burst open, and through them hustled a full score of husky Subversive Scouts. They came to attention and saluted first Freddy Zieglar and then the National Executive Committee Members.

Freddy pointed at the two IBI agents and rapped, "They've both got guns. Disarm them, put handcuffs on them, and haul them off with the others."

"Yes, Comate Commander."

The Scouts went into action.

Bauer was staring at Dick Oppenheimer. He snarled, "Why, you goddamned traitor!"

"Yeah," Dick said sardonically. "A traitor to old man Hardenberg and the IBI, an outfit that would attempt a dirty deal like this. The mistake you made was in not believing me when I told Karen I'd been converted to the Subversive Party. Haul 'em away boys. Take the whole batch of them down to the street and turn them loose. Then go through the building and round up all other so-called Subversive Security men and do the same."

Dick looked at Freddy. "How many Subversive Scouts have you got here in the National Office? I didn't give you much time to muster them."

"About a hundred," Freddy said. "The biggest and best trained guys in the Center City Company."

"Good work," Dick said.

Freddy saluted him and left, in a hurry to take command of his Scouts.

Morris, Karen, Jed and Jack were sitting as though frozen to their chairs, their mouths agape. Jack was the first to partially recover.

"What in the name of the Holy Jumping Zoroaster is going on?" he blurted.

Dick sank back into his chair.

He said, "They were IBI hatchetmen. Department of Dirty Tricks as we call it. Old associates of mine. They were given orders this morning to liquidate the Triumvirate— and you too, Karen. I suggest that as soon as you get in touch with Ted Black that he go on the air and advise all Party members, everywhere, that the so-called Subversive Security men are all really IBI agents and that all of them have been expelled from the Party."

"All of them?" Karen said unbelievingly.

"All of them."

Jack got up and went over to the autobar and said, "I'll buy a drink."

**THE LIFE OF KIT CARSON** **LB474ZK** **$1.25**
**John S.C. Abbott** **Golden West Series**

Christopher "Kit" Carson was a legend to his countrymen. Trapper, trailblazer, scout, and Indian fighter, Kit Carson would become part of American history at its most exciting time—the pioneering of the wild west.

**THE YOKE AND THE STAR** **LB475TK** **$1.95**
**Tana de Gamez** **Novel**

"This tense, compassionate novel has an animal warmth and female ferocity that is very moving indeed."

—*Kirkus Review*

"Expert story-telling, excitement and suspense."

—*Publishers Weekly*

Cuba was ready to explode into bloody revolution. Hannan, the American newsman, could feel the tension in the air, in the eyes of the people in the streets and cafes. Everybody was taking sides; there could be no neutrals in the coming conflict. Hannan thought he could stay out of it. He was wrong. Love for a beautiful revolutionary pushed him past the point of no return.

**THE RETURN OF JACK THE RIPPER** **LB476KK** **$1.75**
**Mark Andrews** **Novel**

An English acting company opened a Broadway play based on the bloody Ripper murders of 1888. Just as the previews began, a prostitute was found dead in a theatre alley—disembowelled, her throat slashed. Other murders followed, and soon the city was gripped in terror. Had the most monstrous figure in the annals of crime returned to kill again?

**THE RED DANIEL** **LB477DK $1.50**
**Duncan MacNeil** **Adventure**

The Royal Strathspey's, Britain's finest regiment, are dispatched to South Africa to take command in the bloody Boer War and find the most fabulous diamond in all of South Africa—The Red Daniel.

**SLAVE SHIP** **LB478KK $1.75**
**Harold Calin** **Adventure**

This is the story of Gideon Flood, a young romantic who sets sails on a slave ship for a trip that would change his life. He witnesses the cruelty of African chieftains who sell their own for profit, the callousness of the captains who throw the weak overboard, and his own demise as he uses an African slave and then sells her.

**A SPRING OF LOVE** **LB479KK $1.50**
**Celia Dale** **Novel**

"A fascinating story."

—*The Washington Star*

"An immaculate performance . . . unsettling, and quite touching."

—*Kirkus Review*

This sweeping novel chronicles a determined young woman's search for enduring love. No matter where it took her, she followed her heart. The man with whom she linked her fortunes was said to be dangerous, but she knew there could be no one else.

**TIME IS THE SIMPLEST THING** **LB480DK $1.50**
**Clifford D. Simak** **Science Fiction**

Millions of light years from Earth, the Telepathic Explorer found his mind possessed by an alien creature. Blaine was a man capable of projecting his mind millions of years into time and space. But that awesome alien penetrated his brain, and Blaine turned against the world . . . and himself.

**ANNA** **LB458DK $1.50**
**Dagfinn Gronoset** **Non-fiction**

In her eighties, an extraordinary Norwegian woman tells of how, fifty years ago, she was sold into lifelong bondage, of her struggles to support her masters and herself in a mountain wilderness, and of her own triumphant survival as a human being. Originally published by Knopf.

**ONLY ON SUNDAY** **LB459DK $1.50**
**Linda DuBreuil** **Non-fiction**

Here are true stories about one small town's principal figures—the preacher with a past who deserts his wife and runs off with the parish funds, the church deacon and the pianist who carry on an affair made in heaven, and a host of others who feign morality six days a week only to sin on the seventh! A paperback original.

**SATAN'S MANOR** **LB460KK $1.75**
**Mark Andrews** **Novel**

The movie crew came to the decaying mansion to film its story . . . a legend filled with murder, revenge, death. The project was jinxed from the beginning with injury, accidental deaths, and strange events. But what would happen soon would be more horrifying than any special effects man could create! A paperback original.

**BOUNTY HUNTER** **LB461ZK $1.25**
**Aaron Fletcher** **Western**

The Bounty Hunter Series will follow the exploits of Jake Coulter, a ruthless bounty hunter determined to bring his prey in dead or alive . . . at any cost. It is a fast paced, fierce, and realistic western ablaze with all the elements that have made our *Sundance* Series an all time bestseller! A paperback original.